Little Vic

Little Vic

BY DORIS GATES

ILLUSTRATED BY KATE SEREDY

THE VIKING PRESS · NEW YORK

Trade 670-43435-3
VLB 670-43436-1

This book is dedicated to

Charlemae Rollins

and

Clara B. Minger

as a small token of my

appreciation and gratitude

Contents

Little Vic

1. Ginger's Colt

H E WAS born in the blue grass country on a spring morning. When his mother pushed her gentle nose against him he got to his feet. He didn't want to stand up. He was not at all sure about his legs. They didn't feel strong under him. For a minute he stood without moving and looked with surprised brown eyes at this strange new world.

There was not much to see—just the four sides of his box stall, and a thick covering of straw on the floor. He moved one of his tiny hoofs in the straw.

He felt his mother's nose upon his back. It made him brave. He took a step. Then from inside him a new feeling sent a signal into his beautiful little head. It was his stomach telling him that it would like some milk. The colt was hungry. Suddenly he moved closer to his mother's side. His own small nose bumped against her ribs and felt along her side. Then he took one more step. This brought him within reach of his breakfast.

It was about an hour later that a boy came into the barn. He went straight to the box stall where Ginger stood with her new colt beside her.

"Well, old lady," said the boy, his face lighting with joy. "Well!"

He opened the door into the stall and slowly went inside. Ginger moved so that she stood between the boy and the colt.

"Come now, old lady," the boy said. "You know me better than that!"

He stood for a minute watching the horse. Then, on the other side of her, the boy could hear something stirring. He knew it was Ginger's baby and he waited. Soon a little nose peeped out at him from under Ginger's neck. Two small ears were pointed toward him. Two wide eyes stared at this strange two-legged animal. Between the eyes was a white star.

"By all that is wonderful," breathed the boy, "another Victory! Only smaller. Come here, Little Vic."

Victory was the colt's father. He was a son of Man o' War who, some people think, was the greatest race horse of all time. Victory was a great race horse in his own right. And now here was a colt of his with the same wide space between his eyes and with a white star upon it.

The little colt seemed interested in the boy. He edged out from behind his mother. Ginger did not seem to care, so the colt came a step nearer. The boy took a step farther into the stall and put out his hand. But Ginger sniffed the hand and blew loudly. It was a warning to the colt, who understood it as such. He quickly backed up under his mother's neck again.

The boy smiled and lowered his hand. He went

13

out of the stall and closed the door. Then he rested his arms on the top of it and looked at Ginger and her son. You could tell from the way he looked at them that he thought they were the two most beautiful things in the world.

"Take your time, old lady," he said to Ginger. He kept his voice low and quiet. "He has a large number of things to learn about this big old world. You're wise to make him take it easy. I'm glad, though, that I'm the first person he ever set eyes on. I'm going to be glad about that for as long as I live."

The boy's name was Jonathan Rivers, but nobody ever called him that. When his mother was alive and feeling cross, she would say "Jonathan" in a special way. But she was gone now, and the name was lost to him for good. It didn't matter, though. From the time he could walk almost, he had been known as "Pony." Pony Rivers was now his name. It suited him, for Pony cared nothing about anything except horses. There were those in the blue grass country who said that he was part horse. Sometimes Pony himself wondered if it were not so. He could not remember when he had not loved horses. He thought he must have come into the world loving them. Sometimes he was sure that he could understand what they would have said if they could talk. And he knew what they were thinking better than he knew what people were thinking.

Pony Rivers had come to Spring Valley Farm about six months ago. He had arrived one stormy night when the rain beat against the windows of the big house and the wind blew puffs of smoke now and then down the big chimney. He had come on a freight train from New York. He had come on the freight because he had no money with which to buy a seat on a passenger train. All the clothes he had were on his back, and they were wet through.

He had spent that first night curled up in a corner of the barn. One of the farm hands had found him there asleep the next morning. He had taken Pony to the man who ran the farm, and the man had not been glad to see the boy.

"What do you mean by hiding in our barn?" Mr. Barby had asked him.

"I was not hiding," said Pony. "I just wanted to get out of the rain until morning. Then I planned to ask you for a job."

Mr. Barby looked at him, and he didn't like what

he saw. The boy standing before him was a little fellow. He didn't look more than twelve years old at
first sight. But there was a fine down on his chin and
an old tired look in his eyes. Mr. Barby decided that
he was perhaps three years older than twelve.

"What is your name?" he asked.

"Pony Rivers," said the boy.

"That is not a name," said the man.

"It's my name," answered the boy.

"How come you have a name like that?"

"It's because I like horses so much. Horses are all
I care about. That's why I came down here to the
horse country. To the blue grass. I want to live all
my days with horses."

"But you said you were from New York. How
could you get to know anything about horses up
there?"

"My father rode race horses until he was killed in
a race. Then my mother took in roomers. Most of
them worked around the race track. They used to
let me go there with them every chance I got. They
taught me things about horses and riding. A month
back I lost my mother. I lived with an aunt after that,
but I didn't like it. She wanted me to get a job selling

papers. I tried that and I didn't like any part of it. So I ran away. I had heard about this country. I knew the great horses came from here. So I decided to head this way. I dropped off the freight about two miles south of here. I came straight to this place."

"Why?"

"Because I knew that Victory was at this farm."

Mr. Barby looked long and thoughtfully at the boy who waited before him. He looked as if he might have been the son of a race-track rider. He was small. He had a quiet way about him that would go well around horses. Perhaps everything was just as he had said.

"Okay," said Mr. Barby at last. "We'll give you a try. But I won't pay you much. You got to show me you know something about horses first."

"I don't care about the pay," said Pony.

Six months had now gone by. In that time Pony Rivers had more than earned his pay. Though he was young he had a way with horses. He thought of nothing else. He was happy only when he was around them. Sometimes Mr. Barby wondered if Pony Rivers was not a little queer about horses. It was he who first said that Pony was part horse.

Spring Valley Farm was one of the biggest farms

in the blue grass country. It was known far and wide
for its fine string of race horses. Each spring a new
crop of colts was born at Spring Valley Farm. Many
of them were the sons and daughters of the farm's
greatest treasure, Victory. In the days before he left
the track, Victory had been the best-known horse in
the country next to his father, Man o' War. It was believed that any colt of his would be a great race horse
too. And so his colts were always watched with interest as they grew old enough to train. As colts, they
brought large prices in the market. Many of his sons
and some of his daughters had already made their
marks in the racing world. Spring Valley Farm could
be very proud of Victory.

It was because of Victory that Pony Rivers had left
the freight at the very spot he did six months back.
He had known for years about Spring Valley Farm.
He had known that here was where Victory belonged. He had seen Victory race. Pony's father had
always hoped that someday he would have a chance
to ride Victory, but the chance had never come. Pony's
father had not been a great rider and had never ridden
any great horses. But he had talked to his small son
about riding and had told Pony many good things

to know. After he was killed, Pony's mother had talked to him against racing. She had tried to make Pony see that there were other ways of living around horses. Pony didn't care if he never became a rider. All he wanted was to live and work with horses. And he decided, as long as he wanted to live on a horse farm, to choose the one where Victory lived.

Now here he was, the first person to be looking at a new son of Victory's. It was the first of his colts to be born at the farm since Pony Rivers had arrived. Pony thought there could never be a more promising colt born anywhere than the lovely little animal he was watching.

After a while he left the barn and went up to the big house. Mr. Barby was there.

"Ginger has her colt," said Pony, very proud to be the first one to spread the good news.

"Are they both all right?" asked Mr. Barby.

"I'll say they are," said Pony. His eyes were shining so that Mr. Barby had to smile. "He's a ringer for his dad. Looks just like Victory, only smaller."

Mr. Barby's smile grew wider. "Sounds like a lucky break for the farm," he said. "And the first one of the season too."

"He's a real little Victory, all right," said Pony. He was watching Mr. Barby's face closely as he said it. But the man seemed not to have heard.

Pony Rivers knew that naming the horses on such a farm as Spring Valley was a very important job. It was always done by the owner or the owner's wife. Then the names had to be given to the people who make the rules about racing in America. He knew that a race horse's name is almost as important as a person's. But he had called the new colt "Little Vic," and he knew that, for him, Little Vic would always be his name.

"Don't you think 'Little Vic' would be a good name for him, Mr. Barby?"

Pony would never know what made him say it. He felt foolish the minute the words were out. He wished with all his heart that he could call them back. He was afraid Mr. Barby would think he was getting too full of himself. He didn't know what Mr. Barby might say to him. Suppose he had made Mr. Barby mad enough to fire him!

But all Mr. Barby did was to look at Pony in a surprised way, and all he said was, "Let's take a look at the colt."

Pony let out a thankful breath and never said another word all the way to the barn.

Mr. Barby was not very well pleased with Ginger's baby, however. "He looks small," he said, tipping his head to one side and looking at the colt out of the tail of his eye. "He looks small. But then you can't always tell. Some of them, born big, don't shape up well later. Time will tell."

"But don't you think he looks just like Victory?" Pony asked.

Mr. Barby tipped his head to the other side. The colt stared back at him as if waiting for his answer. "Yes," said the man slowly. "He has the same dark coat and the star. But there was something different about Victory when he was born. Can't seem to remember just what it was. Something about the way he held his head perhaps, the flash of his eye. This little fellow doesn't seem to have quite as much class."

He turned to look at the boy standing beside him. It was clear that Pony had stopped listening a good many words back. Now he was just feasting his eyes on the lovely colt. He didn't know it, but a smile was playing around his mouth. He looked like a person who is seeing something wonderful, something that no other person can quite see.

"You look as if you've fallen hard for this colt," said Mr. Barby.

Pony jumped. He had forgotten the man at his side. "Yes," he said quietly. "He's the most beautiful thing in this world."

Mr. Barby laughed and slapped Pony on the back. "All right then. If you feel that way about him, I'll turn him over to you. From this day until he starts training, he's going to be your own special care. See that you do a good job with him."

It had been a long time since Pony's eyes had known tears. And then they had not been happy ones. But now tears were once more filling them, though the boy tried hard to fight them back. Through them, the walls of the box stall became all wavy and Ginger and her colt looked wavy too. When at last he thought it was safe to speak, his words sounded foolish to him.

"Do you mean it?" he said, and wiped his eyes with the back of his hand.

"Sure, I mean it," said Mr. Barby. He waited a minute for Pony to get hold of himself. "Doc will be along to check them over." He took a quick look at

Pony. "Ginger kind of put one over on Doc, didn't she? He wasn't expecting the colt for another week."

Pony Rivers said nothing, but he was thinking, as Mr. Barby walked out of the barn, It wasn't Ginger who put one over. It was Little Vic. He isn't ever going to do anything the way people think he will. But he's going to be great just the same!

2. The Naming

THE leaves had grown out on the trees. They were a young light green. Robins were singing among their branches. Soon the birds would be building their nests there. Down in the pasture the new grass was un-rolling a green carpet over the brown earth. The sun was warm. From the open rolling hills came the sound of tractors. They were at work again, turning up to the sun the earth which had been packed down by the winter snow and rain. Behind the tractors, clouds of blackbirds settled upon the moist, newly turned ground to look for earthworms.

Every morning when the dew was gone Pony Rivers led Ginger along the lane which went from the barn to the pasture. Running at her side and kick-ing his small hoofs into the air, her colt followed. All day the two stayed there. Sometimes, tired from play, the colt would curl up in the sun at his mother's feet and sleep. When he woke up, he would eat hungrily while his mother stood quietly. Now and then she would swing her long tail lazily to brush away any fly that might be troubling her baby.

There were other colts in the pasture with their mothers. Ginger's son played with them. Their play was always the same. They would kick and nibble and run in the way colts have always done since time began.

Often Pony came and perched on top of the pasture

fence to watch them. Sometimes there would be a little worried look on his face. There was no getting around it. His favorite was smaller than the other colts. Not much, but a little. Victory was a big horse with powerful shoulders and long legs. Pony knew it was not always the largest horses who make the best racers, but a big strong body is an important thing to a race horse. Pony wanted Little Vic to be big and powerful like his father.

Sometimes when the colt saw Pony sitting there, he would trot toward him. But he would not go up to the fence unless Ginger came too. Usually she did, for Pony always had something in his pockets for her. The boy was waiting for the time when the colt would be as friendly as Ginger, and he knew the time would come. But for some strange reason Little Vic was in no hurry to become close friends with Pony. The other colts would crowd around him when he came into the pasture, but Little Vic always happened to be standing so that his mother's body was between him and the boy.

He's different, thought Pony. He does not give his heart so easily as the others. He does his own thinking, and that is one reason I think he's special.

26

The colt was a month old when the owner of the farm and his wife dropped in at Spring Valley Farm for a visit. Sitting on the pasture fence, Pony Rivers saw a group of people coming toward him down the lane. The women were all dressed in gay colors, and they made a pretty picture as they came talking and laughing down the sun-spotted lane to see the new crop of colts. Mr. Barby was with them. One of the women carried a little dog in her arms. This was Mrs.

Gray, the wife of the owner, but Pony didn't know that yet.

As their voices reached the horses feeding in the pasture, every head was lifted and every ear was pointed at the strangers. The colts stopped their play and ran to their mothers. Every eye was round and fixed on the people coming toward them. Pony jumped off the fence and would have run away, but Mr. Barby called to him.

"Go in and bring Ginger over here, Pony. Mr. Gray wants a look at her colt."

Without a word Pony opened the gate and went inside. The horses stood watching his every move. Straight up to Ginger he went, caught her, and started to lead her toward the group waiting at the gate. Behind her the colt came slowly, as if he wasn't quite sure that he wanted to follow.

Pony had almost reached the gate when suddenly the small dog in Mrs. Gray's arms jumped to the ground, shot under the gate, and started toward Ginger's colt. It was a mean little dog and its bark was sharp and frightening.

"Come here," called Mrs. Gray in a voice that rose as loud as a peanut whistle above the barking. "Come back, Baby. Oh, dear, oh, dear, I know those horses will kill him!"

Pony could hardly believe his ears. The silly woman was worried about her dog when she should have been worried about the colt. After all, the dog had not needed to come into the pasture. He had done it all on his own. And he was now barking and snapping at Ginger's colt. Well, he wasn't going to keep that up very long, thought Pony. Anyway, not while he was around!

He let go of Ginger and dived for the dog. He missed. Ginger rose up on her hind feet and the colt took off for the far side of the pasture. The other mares, who until now had been interested only in watching what went on, became excited for the safety of their own colts. They began to run in wide circles. Somewhere in the mix-up of their pounding hoofs was the dog named Baby.

By the time Pony caught up with him, Ginger's colt had run as far as the pasture fence would let him. There he stood pressed into the fence corner, the little dog dancing from side to side in front of him and barking wildly. The colt's eyes showed white and his sides were going in and out from the excitement of the chase. His nose was wide and pointing low at the dog, and he was blowing loudly and stamping his small front feet. Pony longed to go up to him and lay his hands on his back. There were words he longed to say into his stiff little ears, things that would drive away his frightened look. Pony was sure Little Vic would let him come close this time. But there was still the dog. Baby! Of all the names he had ever heard . . .

And then a new thought rushed into Pony's head. The same woman who had wished that name onto a dog, even *this* dog, might pick a name for Victory's son. Pony's own Little Vic might have to live and race under such a name as Sugar Pie or Honey! Pony couldn't bear to think of it. And yet he knew it had happened to horses before now. It could happen again. He didn't see how any horse could be great if it had a silly name. Yet what could he do about it? he asked himself. Nothing. There was just nothing he could do.

He reached down and picked up the little dog. It growled and tried to bite him. But Pony held it tight by the long hair on its neck, and it could not reach him with its flat nose.

It was a very unhappy boy who came back across the pasture, the little dog in his arms. He didn't see

The Naming

Ginger run to her colt. He didn't know that the horses bunched together behind him began slowly to follow after him. He didn't see Ginger's colt working his way through the bunch to watch where Pony was going. All he saw was the crowd of people at the gate. All he heard was the high, excited voice of Mrs. Gray.

"Oh, you brave, brave boy," she was saying. "You saved Baby from being killed. I saw it all, and I want to give you something. You ran after that wild colt that was trying to stamp on my dear little dog, and you saved him. Ducky," she rattled on, turning to her husband, "I want you to make him out a check for a hundred dollars right away. I would not take ten times that much for Baby."

She had rushed up as soon as Pony was through the gate and had taken the dog into her own arms. Now she held Baby to her face and talked to him in such a silly way that Pony had to turn away from her. He caught Mr. Barby's eye. He could not be sure, but it seemed to Pony that Mr. Barby let one lid fall quickly over one eye, and the look on his face was about like the one Pony could feel on his own. It was clear that Mr. Barby was no happier with these goings-on than Pony. What the boy didn't understand was

how a man who owned a horse like Victory could
have such a silly woman for his wife.

He was about to walk away when suddenly Mrs.
Gray left off loving Baby to remember Pony.

"I can't thank you enough," she was saying. "I just
don't know what I can do to thank you for saving
Baby. Ducky, *do* make out that check."

Mr. Gray was reaching into a coat pocket. Pony
could feel his face getting warm. Everyone was looking at him as if he had done something wonderful—
that is, everyone except Mr. Barby and Mr. Gray. Mr.
Barby realized how Pony felt about Baby. And Mr.
Gray was not happy to be passing out so much money
to anyone for saving Baby. He didn't think any more
of his wife's dog than did Pony and Mr. Barby. But
his wife had told him to do so. What else could he
do, with her and her friends looking on? Mr. Gray
was a very rich man. He didn't want to look small
before these people.

Pony had never felt so uncomfortable in all his life.
He knew he had not really earned anything by "saving" Baby. He didn't think Mrs. Gray should even
thank him for returning the dog to her. He would like
to have thrown Baby to the lions. He had only picked

up the crazy dog to get it out of the colt's neighborhood. A dog like that was nothing to have around horses. Some dogs, all right. But not a barking, biting, snapping little animal like this one. The colt might never get over being afraid of dogs for the rest of his days. Whenever he saw one on a track or near it, he might lose his head. You could not tell about such things. Race horses were mighty touchy animals. The more he thought about it, the angrier he got. Right now he would like to give this Baby a good swift kick. And, feeling that way, he had to stand there like a simpleton and watch Mr. Gray reach into his pocket for his checkbook.

All at once Mr. Barby spoke. "I think I know of something Pony would rather have than a hundred dollars," he said.

Mr. Gray's hand stopped halfway to his pocket, and Mrs. Gray let out a kind of squeak.

"Don't tell me," she cried, "that his name is really Pony! My dear, that is too wonderful."

She looked at Pony as if he might have just dropped from the moon. Poor Pony didn't know what to do. What in the world was Mr. Barby talking about? He had never told him about wanting anything. Not, anyway, since he had got this job of taking care of Ginger and her colt. He had enough to eat and a good bed in the house where the farm hands slept. He had all the clothes he needed. What would he do with a hundred dollars? And what was Mr. Barby talking about?

"What is it you want so much?" Mr. Gray asked him.

Pony looked helplessly at Mr. Barby, and the man understood. He smiled at Pony and spoke for him.

"That colt out there," he began, "the one you wanted most to see, Mr. Gray. Ginger's colt. He's a special favorite of Pony's. He has even given him a name. I think Pony would be the happiest fellow in the world if you would let him name that colt for keeps."

Mr. Gray cleared his throat. "What name did you want to give the colt?" he asked.

Pony swallowed to get his heart out of his mouth. "Little Vic," he said.

Mr. Gray turned the words over in his head. At last he spoke. "I think I like that," he said. "*Little Vic*. Not bad at all. He's the son of Victory, so Little Vic

34

fits him very well. Put that down in the book, Barby. See you later, Pony."

He turned away from the pasture gate and the boy who was propping himself against it. Already the others were going back up the lane. Mrs. Gray was talking sweet talk to Baby while the others were expressing themselves on the danger he had just come through.

Pony watched them out of sight and wondered how it could be that people who cared so little about horses could own such fine ones.

"I guess it takes all kinds of people to make a good world," he said out loud. "If that woman had not been just the kind of person she is, and if that dog had not been just the kind of dog he is, then Little Vic might have had the silliest name in the world. You just can't ever tell about things, I guess."

He turned around and let his eyes travel across the pasture until they found Ginger and the small dark colt at her side. He drew in a deep breath and let it out slowly.

"Little Vic," he said. "Little Vic."

From where he stood safely beside his mother,

Little Vic

Little Vic watched the boy by the gate. A new idea was taking shape in the colt's head. Until today he had thought that only his mother could save him from danger. But today someone else had saved him—that two-legged animal down by the gate. From now on Pony Rivers was going to be very important to this colt whose name was Little Vic.

3. A New Owner

"Easy does it, boy."
Little Vic and Pony were in the colt's stall.
Little Vic was growing up. He was nearly a year old
now and was beginning to look like a race horse. His

eyes were brown and deep and quiet. Sometimes the other colts' eyes flashed their whites when they grew excited or jumpy. But Little Vic never seemed to get excited about anything. He would run and kick and lay his ears back when another colt kicked at him in the pasture. And he would throw up his lovely head and point his ears and swell his nose out with interest when he saw something strange and new to him. But he didn't have a mean hair in his whole body, and his eyes showed how gentle he was.

"Easy does it, boy."

Pony's voice was low and slow. He was feeling down Little Vic's strong front legs. The bone felt light, even thin, under his fingers. But Pony knew that Little Vic's legs were strong as a wire is strong. The colt lifted one foot and pawed the barn floor. He looked almost as if he were trying to shake hands with the boy. But Pony knew it was just that Little Vic didn't like having his legs rubbed. He had always been touchy about it, ever since he was a little fellow.

After Pony had looked carefully at each front foot, he moved to the back ones. Again Little Vic showed how little he liked this kind of thing. But he never tried to kick Pony. He would just lift his foot high, then set it down hard.

The boy and the colt had become good friends since that afternoon when Little Vic had received his name. Now when Pony entered the pasture where Little Vic was running, the colt would know it at once and come racing toward him. And Pony always had a piece of carrot ready for him.

No other person on the farm thought of doing anything for Little Vic. Everyone understood the deep love which had grown up between the two. It was almost as if the colt had become the boy's very own. Mr. Barby sometimes laughed at Pony's great love for this son of Victory. Then he would look at Pony in a troubled way. At last one day he spoke to the boy of the danger of loving Little Vic too much. "It will make it harder to lose him later on," the man said kindly.

Pony looked surprised. "What do you mean?" he asked.

"I think Little Vic is one of the colts that Mr. Gray means to sell next spring."

"But Little Vic is the son of Victory," Pony said. "He'll be a great horse someday."

Little Vic

Mr. Barby narrowed his eyes at the colt and looked at him carefully. "That may well be," he answered. "But that colt is small. I don't think we'll keep him."

Now for the first time in a long time Pony was worried. He had not thought about the chance that the colt would be sold. He had even got to thinking of the colt as his very own. But from that day when Mr. Barby warned him of the danger, Pony felt fear like a dull pain eating at his heart. From then on he tried to make Little Vic grow more. He wanted more than anything in the world to have the colt race under Mr. Gray's colors. Not that he cared one way or the other about Mr. Gray, but if Mr. Gray owned Little Vic, Pony would be able to stay near him. Or, at least, that's what Pony thought.

Sometimes at night he would wake from dreaming that Little Vic had been taken from him. For a second or two his heart would thump against his ribs, and his eyes, looking into the darkness, would be round with fear. He would tell himself it was only a dream and would try to go back to sleep again. But it never worked. Always he would have to get up and make his way to the colt's stall. There he would run his hands over the warm body, which felt as smooth as silk to his touch. Little Vic would bump him with his soft nose and nip playfully at his friend's shoulder. For the rest of the night Pony would sleep soundly in a corner of the stall, a smile on his face because Little Vic was safely near him.

But while Little Vic kept strong and well under Pony's care, he still didn't grow as much as Mr. Barby wanted him to. By the time the spring sales were due, there were many finer-looking colts on the farm than he.

Then suddenly, without warning of any kind, Little Vic began to get thin. He seemed perfectly well, as far as anyone could see, but he began to have a bony look. His ribs showed and his hip bones stood out. Pony thought it might be that the colt had begun to grow faster, but Mr. Barby wouldn't even listen to him when he tried to tell him this. Instead he just said that Little Vic was among the colts that Mr. Gray had decided to sell.

The colts, four of them, were shipped away to the place where they were to be sold. Pony and another boy rode with them in a special car that had stalls built in it for horses. There was heat and hay in the car, and the horses seemed as happy as in their stalls at home. As usual, Little Vic showed no fear as the train started. He was interested in his new home and looked around him carefully. But Pony laid a hand on his neck, and Little Vic stood quietly, as if he knew the boy would let no harm come to him.

The bidding on the colts took place in a big tent. It was as big as a circus tent. A crowd of men and women were there to see what this spring's crop of one-year-olds looked like. Most of the colts had come from fine stock, and all of them had their names and the names of their parents entered in the records of the racing board. Some of the people in the crowd already owned many race horses. Others had only one or two. A very few people had come to buy their first race horse. And some were there only because they liked horses and wanted to be in on the show.

At last it was Little Vic's turn to be put on the block. Pony didn't feel the eyes of the crowd on him as he led the colt into the squared-off place where the people could get a good look at him. He was worried that Little Vic might be frightened by the strangeness around him. And he was ashamed that his favorite didn't look better. So many beautiful horses had stood in this same spot while the bidding was going on that poor Little Vic made a sorry picture. There were no ohs and ahs as Pony led him out. The people looked at him, talked about his father, and shook their heads to think that Victory's colt should show so little promise.

Suddenly an exciting new thought came to Pony. Maybe Little Vic would not be sold after all! Maybe he looked so bad no one would want to buy him! Maybe they would be going back together to the farm in the blue grass!

But no, the bidding had started. Even though he did look thin and "off," he was Victory's son just the same. Several voices spoke, making offers for Little Vic, while Pony stood sorrowfully by and tried to swallow the lump in his throat. Once Little Vic bumped him playfully, then rubbed his nose along Pony's sleeve, as if to say, "Cheer up, things always turn out for the best." But Pony seemed not to understand what Little Vic was trying to tell him.

At last a man called out, "Five thousand dollars!" No one made a higher bid, so the bidding on Little Vic was closed and the colt had a new owner.

Sadly Pony led him back to his stall. There the boy smoothed the colt's back while he thought things over.

He would have to decide quickly what he was going to do, because any minute now the new owner would be coming along to take his new colt away.

For some reason Pony had got the idea that Little Vic would somehow know and object to having a new owner. It would have made Pony feel better if the colt had acted as if he felt bad too. But Pony's love for Little Vic had made him forget for the moment that

A New Owner

Little Vic was, after all, a horse. So now Little Vic just nibbled at his oats and looked around in quiet surprise when Pony, feeling lonelier than he had ever felt before, crossed his arms on Little Vic's back and laid his head down.

He was still standing this way when the new owner arrived at the stall. Hearing footsteps, Pony made a slap at his eyes, then turned quickly to face the new owner.

"He's not much for looks, is he?" the man said to Pony.

"He's the best," the boy replied in a shaky voice.

The man looked more closely at the boy. "What makes you think so?"

Pony took a deep breath, and when he spoke his voice was almost his own again. "Can't tell for sure. Just something about him. He kind of thinks things out for himself. He isn't mean, ever. There's something about him that says"—here Pony stopped and searched inside him for just the right words—"something that says, 'Just give me time and I'll show you.' "

Pony looked quickly at the stranger, wondering if he might be laughing at him. But the man was looking at the colt, and Pony couldn't be sure that he had even taken the trouble to listen. So Pony took this chance to look over Little Vic's new owner.

He was a small man with dark hair and eyes. He was wearing a gray hat pulled low over his forehead. A long, dark topcoat covered his suit. It was well cut and hugged his shoulders smoothly. His black shoes were shining. On the little finger of his left hand was a gold ring with a blue stone set into it. He looked very fine and rich. But his eyes, as they passed back and forth over Little Vic, were hard, and he made no move to pet the colt.

Soon he was joined by another man, who looked enough like Little Vic's new owner to be his brother. He even wore the same kind of clothes and the same kind of ring.

"Hello, Lefty," said the new man. "Feeling lucky today?"

"Hello, Bill," said Lefty. He moved his head toward the colt. "Had a feeling about him. Think I'll send him down to Jack Baker. He may be able to turn him into a race horse someday."

"Five thousand dollars is a lot of money to take a chance on," Bill said.

Lefty gave a short laugh. "I've lost more than that on one race. Besides he was a good buy. Son of Victory."

"He don't look so good," said the other.

Lefty narrowed his eyes and answered, "I like 'em thin."

Pony Rivers had been listening carefully to the talk. He had seen a lot of men like Lefty and his friend around the race tracks. They were always heavy betters. They made a business of race-track betting. Sometimes they owned a race horse or two. But they cared nothing for the horses. Horses, to them, were just another way of making money quickly and easily. It hurt Pony that Little Vic had been sold to one of these.

As the two were turning to leave, Pony spoke at last. "Mister Lefty, please."

The man turned and looked at Pony, a smile turning up one side of his thin mouth. "What's on your mind?" he asked. He ran the words all together so that they sounded like one word. This was because it was a question he asked many times during the day. Usually people who spoke to him as Pony had just spoken needed some money. Lefty was known in his crowd as a "soft touch." So now he waited to see whether Pony wanted one dollar or five.

It took Pony several seconds to get the answer out, but Lefty waited. He even got a little fun out of watching Pony's struggle. People usually didn't have any trouble leading up to a "touch."

"I'd like to stay with the colt," said Pony.

A line appeared quickly between Lefty's hard eyes. This was not what he had expected, and the unexpected had a way of making him angry. He was not a man who liked being taken by surprise.

"How you mean?" asked Lefty.

"Well, you see, Mister Lefty," Pony began, his eyes watching the man's face for any slightest signal of anger, "it's me that's taken all the care of Little Vic since the morning he was born. He hasn't been handled by anybody but me. And, of course, Mr. Barby," he added, wanting to be quite truthful.

He stopped, and the man looked from Pony to the colt. He seemed to be turning over what Pony had said, so the boy decided to give his chances a telling push.

"I wouldn't want anything but enough to eat and a pair of jeans now and then."

A New Owner

Lefty looked for a long minute into Pony's round, steady eyes. At last he said, "Okay. I'm shipping the colt to Jack Baker's training farm. You go along. And if Jack says you can stay, it's okay by me."

"Thank you, Mister Lefty." Pony's smile was a wonderful thing to see. "I'll take care of him like he was my brother. I promise."

"I want you to take care of him like he was your meal ticket," returned Lefty. "What's your name?"

"Pony Rivers."

Lefty did not seem surprised. There were names even stranger than that in this crowd. He reached into an inside pocket and took out a flat leather billfold. From it he took a five-dollar bill and flipped it toward the boy.

"There'll be a truck along in a little while. If you get the colt into it without his hurting himself and deliver him safe to Jack Baker, there will be another one like that waiting for you when you get there."

Pony took the bill and looked at it without saying a word. It was the first five-dollar bill he had ever owned. He was still looking at it when the men went away. At last his eyes lifted from the greenback to the colt standing beside him. He stuffed the bill into

49

a pocket of his jeans and gently laid his hand along the colt's neck.

"Did you hear him, Little Vic? He said he'd give me another five for getting you there safe. Can you beat that? *Paying* me to see that nothing bad happens to you! Some folks don't understand anything except money, do they?"

To the boy's delight, Little Vic moved his head up and down as if he were agreeing with every word.

4. In Training

LITTLE VIC arrived safely at Jack Baker's training farm, and Pony was allowed to stay there with him. Lefty was as good as his word. When Jack told him over the telephone that the horse had arrived without trouble of any kind, Lefty told him to give the boy five dollars and add it to Little Vic's feed bill.

"The kid seems kind of nuts about the horse," Lefty explained to the trainer. "Maybe it would be all right to let the kid hang around. Is that okay with you, Jack?"

"Sure," Jack said. "I can always use another boy. Especially when they don't want much pay, like this one. And he seems to have a way with horses. He's sure in love with this colt of yours. Won't let him out of his sight."

"What do you think of the colt?" asked Lefty.

"Not bad," said Jack. "It's a good blood line. But he looks off a bit. I'll see if he can run after a while."

"He's your baby," said Lefty. "Do what you need to do and send me the bill. I'm taking a chance on the colt, that's all. If he works out, fine. If he don't—so he don't, that's all."

"You can count on me," Jack told him. "If he's got anything in him, I'll find it."

The next day Little Vic's training began.

He had already learned a few things. Pony had taught him to follow quietly at the end of a rope. The colt was gentle and willing. In no time he was carrying a saddle without irons, and not seeming to object to it so very much. He kicked at first when Pony pulled up the saddle bands around his middle. And when that didn't loosen them, Little Vic bucked a few times. But Pony spoke quietly to him and just let him buck. After a few hard jumps Little Vic seemed to catch on to the fact that the bands were not really hurting him at all. They didn't even feel as tight as they had at first. He stopped bucking and looked at Pony, and Pony grinned at him. Little Vic blew a long, strong breath out of his nose and pawed at the ground with a small front foot. Pony knew what that meant. He pulled a carrot from his pocket and gave it to the colt. The next minute Little Vic was eating his carrot as happily as if he had never seen a saddle. The next day when Pony put the saddle on him Little Vic just looked around for the carrot that went with it and never bucked at all.

Now that Little Vic had learned to wear a saddle and had found out what it was like to have a bit in his mouth, he was to know what it was like to have a man on his back. Or at least a boy. For Jack Baker had decided to let Pony Rivers be the first person to sit on Little Vic's shiny back.

"This won't be so easy," Jack Barber warned the

boy. "Little Vic seems to like to buck, and he's sure going to do just that when you hit the saddle. He may throw you, so be prepared."

"I don't care what he does to me," said Pony, "if only he can do it to me first. I mean, no matter what he does to me, I want it to be me he does it to and not some other fellow. I'm not going to get mad at him, and some other fellow might. I'll know it's just because he's new to all this and doesn't know any better. Because Little Vic wouldn't ever be bad on purpose. He has never done a mean thing since he was born."

"I hope you're right," said Jack Baker as if he didn't quite believe all Pony said. "But I've handled a lot of horses in my time, and some race horses can be as mean as they come. Even when they don't act that way on purpose."

Pony took a lot of time getting Little Vic used to having a heavy weight on his back. At first Pony tried to hook his arms over the colt's backbone and let him feel the weight of his body across his back. Each time he did this Little Vic would step to one side quickly, and Pony would slip to the ground. Slowly and without ever becoming angry, Pony would walk up to the colt and pat him before trying once again to place his full weight across Little Vic's back.

One day when Pony flung himself lightly against the colt's side, Little Vic did not move. Pony hung for a minute. Still Little Vic did not move. So Pony gave a little spring, and now his body was right across the colt's back. And the colt was not moving! The boy could feel Little Vic's body shaking under him, so in just a minute he let himself down slowly to the ground again. Then he patted Little Vic's smooth neck and gave him a carrot. It wasn't long after that before Pony could climb onto Little Vic's bare back any time he wanted to, and the colt never seemed to object. From that it was only a step to riding him with a saddle. And one proud day Jack Baker, with Pony up, led the colt to the training track along with several others.

"Did you ever ride a fast horse before?" Jack Baker asked the boy.

"No, sir," Pony replied. "But my father did. He told me lots about racing."

"Remember all he told you," said Jack. "You may need it someday. But for now I just want to see the colt work. I don't care about speed. Not this morning.

Don't try to pour it on. Just let him go as he wants to go."

"Yes, sir," said Pony. He could hardly get the words out, his teeth were knocking together so hard. Beyond any doubt, this was the most exciting moment of his whole life, Pony was telling himself as Little Vic walked quietly along. Once he had dreamed of a moment like this, but he had never really thought it would come true. He was going to ride Little Vic on a track, and for all future time people would have to remember when the great son of Victory was mentioned, that he, Pony Rivers, was the *first* person ever to ride him!

Of course the track was not a real race track. It was hardly more than a riding ring. But it was a large one, and it had two white fences between which the colts would work out.

They came to the opening in the fence which let them onto the track. A man on a pony started first, and the four colts came after him. The pony was really a horse, but all horses around race tracks are called ponies when they are not racers but old and settled and quiet horses. At first the pony led them at a walk. Pony Rivers sat with his knees high up on

In Training

Little Vic's saddle and watched the play of his shoulders as he moved. Pony held the colt lightly but with enough weight on the bit so that Little Vic should know that he was there and ready for whatever might happen.

Suddenly the pony out in front of them was trotting, and the colts began to trot too. Pony Rivers rose in the saddle to Little Vic's trot. The colt pointed his ears and tossed his head and pulled against the bit. Little Vic wanted to go faster! Pony smiled to himself. But he knew better than to give the colt his head. If he went against Jack Baker's orders, he knew very well that he would never be allowed to ride Little Vic again. And it would serve him right too, Pony told himself. The way a horse is handled during his early training can make or break him as a race horse. And it is for the trainer to decide how a horse should be handled. So now Pony held Little Vic close and kept him to a trot.

They trotted the full circle back again to where Jack Baker was waiting. He looked at each of the colts and felt them down. When he came to Little Vic he said, "What made him throw his head up over on the far side when you started to trot?"

Pony shook his head. "I don't know," he said, "unless it was because he wanted to run. Don't forget, he's the son of Victory," he said proudly, just as if Jack Baker didn't already know.

"He'll get his chance all in good time," said the trainer. "Take him back to the stable and walk him out."

"Yes, sir," said Pony, and they started for the barn.

In front of the stable Pony walked Little Vic around and around until he had cooled off from his morning workout.

Each day Little Vic's workouts became longer. Sometimes he ran with a number of colts and sometimes he worked alone. Jack Baker trained him to run on the fence—that is, Pony was told to keep Little Vic working close to the fence because during a race the jockeys try to keep on the inside fence in order to save distance.

The colts were also taught to walk up to the fence, then to back straight away from it. This was to teach them how to act when the day came that they had to stand in the starting gate before a race. The starting gate is like a row of stalls. Each stall is closed at one end, and kept closed until the moment for the race to start. Then the stall is opened in a flash, the horses are sent bounding forward by their jockeys, and the race is on.

The months went by, and Little Vic showed more promise with every week that passed. To Pony's great joy, the colt lost his thin look. He began to fill out. His long legs gave promise of great speed. His quiet manner made him easy to handle. But he had begun to hold his head very high and proud, like a king. When he came out of the stable for his early morning workout his head was always high, his ears pointed forward, and his eyes seemed fixed on something far off that only he could see.

One morning Pony leaned forward on the colt's neck and whispered to him, "What is it you see, fellow? Is it the Gold Cup shining way out there ahead somewhere? Is it the heap of prize money you are going to win one of these days? Maybe it's a new track record you see set up on a board in the sky away out there. That would be the best yet. A new world's record. A great horse. Can you feel it in your bones already, Little Vic?"

That morning as he rode the colt around the track Pony dreamed that he was wearing the brightly colored silks of some great stable and that Little Vic, with Pony up, was breaking the wire in front of a roaring grandstand.

Jack Baker was waiting for him at the gate. His face was dark with anger. "You let that colt run like that again and you're through. Understand? I thought I could trust you. What came over you anyway?"

Pony hung his head while his heart thumped with sudden fear. "I'm sorry," he said very low.

"What happened?" the trainer asked. "Did the colt make a break? Couldn't you handle him?"

Pony's answer came quick and sure. "Oh, no, Mr. Baker," he said, "Little Vic didn't do anything bad. It was my fault. He just felt good, that was all, and so when he started to run, I guess—why I guess I just forgot to hold him in." He paused, then added, "I got to thinking I was in a race."

The anger slowly went out of Jack Baker's face. He felt the colt down carefully, then he put a hand on Pony's knee and looked up at him. "Kid," he began, "it's bad business when an exercise boy begins to think he's a jockey. When you take a colt out to work him, you must remember you're not racing him. And you are not a jockey."

In Training

"Yes," said Pony, still afraid that Mr. Baker might change his mind and fire him after all.

"But you know, Pony," the trainer went on, and now his voice had changed. It had become a friendly voice. He was talking to Pony as the boy's father might have talked to him. "You know, Pony, I've been watching you pretty close the last few weeks. You have good hands, and until this morning you've had a good head. You know horses very well for a kid your age. And you are very small for your age. Did you ever think about becoming a jockey?"

Pony's eyes were shining and for a moment he could not say a word. The trainer started to walk toward the stables, and Pony rode Little Vic at a walk beside him. At last he said in a wondering voice, "Do you think I could ever be a jockey, Mr. Baker?"

"Why not?" asked the man.

"Gee," was all Pony could say. Then he turned toward the man so suddenly that Little Vic danced a few side steps and Pony had to quiet him. "Do you think, Mr. Baker, that Mr. Lefty would let me ride Little Vic when he decides to start him?"

Mr. Baker laughed but not unkindly. "Well, hardly that, Pony. A boy can't expect to start out riding

61

horses like Little Vic. You have to knock around small races like they have at country fairs, and things like that. Or you have to start with horses that have seen their best days. The kind of horses that the first-class jockeys don't want to ride. A horse like this colt here is too fine to trust to a new rider. You can understand that, can't you?"

"I guess so," said Pony, but he didn't sound as if he really thought so. Then a new idea struck him. "But Little Vic has never had anyone on him but me. It stands to reason that he would go better for me than for somebody he never saw before."

"It's one thing to ride a horse in a workout and it's another thing to ride the same horse in a race," Jack Baker told him. "You've got to have some experience before an owner will trust you with a horse like Little Vic. But you will be a fine jockey one of these days, Pony. If I were you I would start in at the country fairs this summer, riding in the short races. You can learn a lot and get to be known doing that. By next year you could be riding really good horses. Think it over."

They had reached the stables and Pony had slid from the saddle. "I don't have to think it over, Mr.

Baker. I'd rather be Little Vic's exercise boy than
Man o' War's jockey, if Man o' War were alive."

Jack Baker looked at Pony, smiled, and shook his
head. "I've heard of fellows like you, Pony, who fell
in love with a horse. But remember, they can break
your heart the same as a woman. I only hope Little
Vic never lets you down. You're just storing up
trouble for yourself, son."

Pony stood thinking for a moment, and when at
last he looked at Jack Baker there was the kind of
smile on his face that showed he was very sure of himself. "The way I see it, Mr. Baker, everybody has got
to have some trouble in this world. I just got the feeling I would rather have the kind of trouble Little Vic
will pick out for me than any other trouble I can think
of. And you know something?" Pony moved so that
he could look into the colt's eyes. "The way I see it,
as long as I can be with Little Vic, nobody can hand
me any trouble anyway."

All Jack Baker said was, "Maybe you got something
there," and walked away without telling Pony what
was on his mind. As long as Lefty owned Little Vic,
Pony could no doubt stay with him. But Jack Baker
knew that Lefty never held on to anything very long.

He thought it might be kinder to let Pony find this out for himself.

Suddenly there rose before the man's eyes the sight of Little Vic's run on the track this morning, and he began to hurry toward the farm office. Once there he picked up the telephone. He called a number, and when a voice answered he said, "I want to send a wire to Lefty Santo." He gave the address, then waited until the voice at the other end of the wire asked for the message. It was a short one. "You have bought yourself a horse," said Jack Baker into the telephone.

5. The Meet

BY THE next January Little Vic was a two-year-old and ready to prove himself on the race tracks of America. Lefty decided to enter him in a meet in Florida. The colt, along with Pony Rivers, was therefore shipped to Florida along with several others Jack Baker was taking there for training.

Now for the first time Little Vic and Pony did their workouts every morning on a real race track. When Jack thought Little Vic was ready, he put him down for a race in which only two-year-olds would run.

It was a great day for Pony Rivers. He was proud and excited. But he was worried too. And for several reasons. For one thing it was Little Vic's first meet. And then Pony didn't like the looks of the boy who had been chosen to ride Little Vic. He looked mean and he seemed to take it for granted that the colt was mean too.

"Every horse in that blood line bites," said Buddy Winkle as he looked over Little Vic for the first time. Buddy Winkle was not quite as new to the track as Little Vic, but he had yet to ride a winning horse. He wanted to ride one very badly, and looking at the colt before him he thought Little Vic might be that horse. But not for the world would he have let the colt's exercise boy know that he, Buddy, thought well of Little Vic. Not Buddy. He wasn't sticking his neck out. No, sir! If this colt made a bad race of it, no one could say it was Buddy's fault. Not if he knew it! Better to let people think you made a good race with a bad horse than a bad race with a good one.

"He don't look like he could win," Buddy said. His eyes as they traveled over the colt looked sharp and sort of hungry.

The Meet

Pony saw the look and hid his smile. He knew what Buddy was thinking. "You don't look so good to me either," he said. "And if you don't like Little Vic I can tell Mr. Lefty and he can maybe get another boy."

Buddy threw a hard look at Pony. "You mind your own business. I've been asked to ride this colt and I'm going to ride him. That don't mean I got to love him." He gave a short laugh and walked quickly away.

Still smiling, Pony led Little Vic back to his stall. Maybe Buddy Winkle was okay after all, he tried to tell himself. Pony wanted to be fair. He remembered hearing some talk about Buddy around the stables. People seemed to think that he was a smart and coming young rider. Maybe, Pony thought, he felt as he did about Buddy because he didn't want anyone but himself to ride Little Vic. Maybe he would feel the same way about any jockey. Maybe Buddy was okay. He would try to think so. The important thing was that Little Vic should win this first race. If Buddy could bring that about, why then Pony might even take back what he had said to him. On second thought, though, he decided he wouldn't go that far. Not after what Buddy had said about Little Vic!

Lefty flew down from New York for the race. If

things went well he might stay for the meet, or at least a large part of it. Racing was an important thing in Lefty's life. The fact that most of the time he got his racing results over the telephone had no effect on his interest in the sport. It was through horse racing and betting that Lefty made most of his money.

Since receiving Jack Baker's wire so many months ago, Lefty had done a lot of talking about his horse. Some of his closest pals had come along with him today to see the colt run for the first time. They had joked with Lefty about his "stable" and thought him a fool to spend so much good money on a horse.

But when they saw Little Vic they changed their tune. He looked like the real thing, and after the colt's workout that morning they thought Lefty had got his money's worth after all. The fourth race that afternoon would prove how right or wrong they were.

Jack Baker gave Buddy a leg up and a few last directions before the horses started to the post. As Pony might have expected, Little Vic was quiet. But he looked carefully at the crowds of people and seemed to take a special interest in the lines of shiny automobiles standing away off in the sunlight of the parking lots. When the fourth race was called he followed quietly in his post position when the man in a bright red coat, riding a gray pony, led the race horses to the starting gate. Little Vic was Number Eight. It took several minutes to get the horses settled in the starting stalls. They had not all had the good handling that Jack Baker gave his colts.

At last the colts were all in line and quiet. Then the gate was opened, and with a rush ten excited colts broke into the open. It was a clean start.

Little Vic had not had time to settle into his speed when there was a fierce roar in the sky over the track. It sounded above the noise of the horses' pounding feet and the cries of the jockeys. At once Little Vic began to slow up. In vain did Buddy Winkle lay on with the whip, in vain did he shout. Little Vic had decided to find out where that noise was coming from and what was making it. He had come almost to a stop when three jet planes roared over him, their long black streamers of smoke floating behind them. Satisfied with what he saw, Little Vic then continued on his way, but the field was well ahead of him. Not even Victory himself could have closed the distance between them. There was a roar of laughter from the stands as Little Vic, a very late last, came past the grandstand. Pony,

hearing the laughter of the crowd and knowing that
it was directed at Little Vic, was glad for once that
his favorite was just a horse and wouldn't understand
what that laughter meant. From his place at the fence
rail the boy watched sadly as horse and rider crossed
the finish line. Suddenly his face drew up into lines
of anger. Buddy Winkle was raising his whip. He
couldn't! He wouldn't dare, Pony tried to tell himself. But he was doing it. Right in front of Pony's eyes,
Little Vic was being struck a hard blow on the head
by an angry rider. And after the finish of a race! Pony
began to run toward Little Vic. Buddy slid from the
saddle, but the judges had seen. Buddy would be fined.
But more than that was to happen to Buddy! He must
first deal with Pony Rivers!

Buddy had just time to say, "I never thought he
could win," before Pony hit him. The jockey tried
to cover up, but Pony was all over him in a flash. Before anyone could stop him, he hit Buddy again, and
blood began to run from the jockey's nose. Now Pony
took a hard right on his mouth, ducked under Buddy's
left, and aimed his own right straight at Buddy's jaw.
It landed with all Pony's strength behind it, and the
jockey dropped to the ground. He didn't get up right

away. At last some men lifted him to his feet, while others kept Pony from doing any further harm. All at once Pony's angry head cleared enough to let him feel a hand on his shoulder squeezing him hard. He turned his head and looked straight up into the face of Lefty Santo.

"I couldn't have done it better," said the man, "and I never lost a fight I didn't throw. You gave him just what he had coming to him, and you were the one to do it. It was worth every dollar I lost on the race. And more besides." Saying which, Lefty reached into his inside pocket as he had once before while Pony looked on. He drew out the leather billfold and from it picked out a greenback. He handed the bill to Pony. "Here," he said with his crooked smile, "ever see one of these before? I've paid 'em for a ringside seat that didn't give me as good a show. It's all yours, kid. And thanks."

Without waiting for Pony's thanks, Lefty walked away, surrounded by his pals. Still unable to believe what he saw, Pony folded the hundred-dollar bill and stuck it in his pocket. Then he hurried to the stable where he felt sure Little Vic would be wondering why he didn't appear.

In a few moments Jack Baker and Lefty came to the colt's stall. Pony was walking him out but stopped when Jack gave him a signal.

"You got to remember it's his first race," Jack Baker was telling Lefty.

"I know all that," said Lefty. "Buddy says the horse just gave up; didn't seem to have no interest in the race at all."

Pony was listening to every word and found it hard to believe his ears. Didn't Lefty know what had happened? Didn't these two men have any understanding of Little Vic at all?

"Mr. Lefty," he said, going over to him, "I know why Little Vic didn't run. That Buddy Winkle don't know anything about a horse like Little Vic."

"What happened, kid?" Lefty asked.

"Those planes," said Pony. "They were making a big noise and he had never heard a noise like that before. So Little Vic slowed up to have himself a look. There was nothing in that race could come close to him if those planes had stayed out of the picture."

Lefty was looking sharply at Pony. "Maybe you got something there, Pony. I remember now, those planes did come over just as the horses broke out of the gate." Then his face darkened again. "That still don't clear Little Vic, though. The other colts kept right on going. What makes him so jumpy?"

Pony was quick with an answer. "Little Vic has never been jumpy and I don't think he's jumpy now. But he has more sense than the others, Mr. Lefty. When he saw something he didn't understand, he just wanted to know more about it. Now he knows jet planes won't hurt him, he'll never be interested in them again. You wait and see."

"You mean I got to wait until he checks off every little thing one by one until some happy day he decides it's about time to settle down and run a race?" Lefty was almost shouting, and men at the other stables had stopped their work to listen to him. Now he turned his anger toward Jack Baker. "And I thought you said I had bought myself a horse! Tell me one thing, Jack—have you ever seen a race horse in your life?"

Jack smiled but not very happily. "Take it easy, Lefty. This has happened before to horses who made good in a big way. Give the colt a chance. Let him train another day or two, then start him again. If that colt can't win, then I never saw one that could."

"Okay," said Lefty, and Pony let out a thankful breath. "Whatever you say. But mark my words, if he don't show me something next time—not a lot, you understand, but *something*—then I'm going to put him in a claiming race and anyone with the price can have him."

Pony began to walk Little Vic again and now he was talking under his breath to the horse. "You hear that, fellow? No foolish business next time. Don't you remember what I've been telling you right along? Nothing out there is ever going to hurt you except another horse. Or a bad jockey. If a horse bangs into you and knocks you down, okay, so you can't run. But nothing else is ever going to hurt you on the track. No matter what you see or think you see, you just keep on going. You understand?"

He looked closely at the colt, who returned the look without giving any sign that he did or did not know what Pony had said.

Though Little Vic had proved to be an "also ran" in his very first race, he drew more attention from the sports writers than most "also rans" ever do. Victory's son was something of a joke when next he went to the post. The big question among the fans was not

The Meet

"could he win?" but "would he run?" The other boys around the stables had many a laugh at Pony's expense. But the boy continued to stand up for his horse.

Another rider had been chosen for Little Vic this time. Jack Baker's last words to him had been, "Don't let him forget for one minute that he's in a race." The jockey had answered, "Leave it to me," as he put Little Vic in the line of horses following the gray pony to the starting gate.

Again Pony Rivers leaned on the white fence, his eyes never leaving the dark brown and beautifully moving colt now approaching the starting gate. Little Vic was Number Six this time in a field of eight two-year-olds.

It had been a long time since Pony Rivers had felt the need of prayer. But now his lips were moving as he kept saying over and over to himself, "Please Lord, let him make a good race of it!" Pony was remembering with terrible clearness what Lefty had said a couple of days ago. If Little Vic failed today, he would be put in a claiming race and anyone meeting the claiming price would become the owner of Little Vic. Pony didn't quite dare hope that the next owner of the colt would take him along too. No one's luck could hold three times in a row. So now he prayed, trying to comfort himself with the thought that God would not let him down, even if by some strange chance Little Vic did.

There was the usual wait until all the horses were in line. Then the moment when they were all in and no one in the grandstand seemed to be breathing, while every eye was on the far side of the track where the horses stood in the starting gate waiting for the moment when it would open. Finally the moment arrived, the gate opened, and eight horses leaped madly forward.

It became clear at once that Little Vic's jockey was indeed ready for anything. To keep the colt from noticing anything which might make him forget that he was in a race, he hit him a hard blow with his whip to start him forward. The blow surprised Little Vic; but, more than that, it angered him. When it was followed immediately by a second, harder blow, the colt went wild. Not since the first time Little Vic had had a saddle fastened to him had he felt such anger. Since he had done nothing to deserve it, there was no reason for him to think that the man on his back would not

continue to beat him all the way around the track.
There was only one thing for the colt to do. He must
get rid of the man on his back. So Little Vic began
to buck. It was a hard, cow-horse buck, and with the
second thudding jump the jockey sailed up and over
Little Vic's head. Then the colt proceeded without his
rider around the track the way the others had gone.
This time the grandstand was wild as Little Vic went
past it with an empty saddle.

Pony had already leaped the fence onto the track,
and now he trotted to catch up with the colt. He
caught him easily, and without waiting for Lefty or
Jack Baker the boy led the colt toward the stables.
There he took off the saddle and began to rub the
colt down. But, as before, his faith in Little Vic was
not shaken.

"He had it coming to him," he told the colt. "You
did just right. I saw him hit you before you had a
chance to show him. You went willing and he hit you.
He had it coming. But oh, Little Vic, what is Mr.
Lefty going to say?"

As once before when Pony had been deeply shaken
about the chances for their future together, Little Vic

just went on nibbling his oats as if he didn't in the least understand that anything was wrong.

Pony never knew what Mr. Lefty had to say, however. The man didn't even bother to come back to the stable to see Little Vic after the race. It was Jack Baker who told Pony the bad news.

"He's sick of the whole business," he told Pony when the boy turned a questioning face to him. "He wants to put the colt in the claiming race for two-year-olds next week. It's for three thousand dollars."

Pony could only swallow and wink very hard.

"And I don't mind telling you, Pony," Jack Baker went on, "that whoever buys Little Vic for three thousand dollars is going to get a lot of horse for the money."

Pony could only nod his head to show he agreed. He didn't want to take a chance on speaking. His voice might give him away.

But Jack Baker seemed to understand. He laid a hand on Pony's shoulder. "I'm sorry your horse let you down, son. Maybe whoever claims him next week will need you too."

Now Pony's voice was firm. "Little Vic won't ever let me down. No matter what happens, Little Vic won't let me down. He knows what he's doing better than anybody could know for him. He's the best there is."

Jack Baker turned away. "I hope you're right, son. I sure hope you are."

6. Pony Has a Plan

THE very next week Little Vic finished out of the money in a claiming race for two-year-olds. It began to look as if Lefty had been right about the colt, after all. Three races and still Little Vic had not shown the stuff he was made of. Something was wrong with him, at least something was wrong with his racing heart.

That is what Jack Baker told Pony, but the boy would not have it that way. "The trouble is, Mr. Baker, Little Vic is just too wise. He knows what this kind of racing is worth, and he won't go for it."

Jack Baker looked at the boy as if he could hardly believe his ears. "What's that again?" he asked.

"Like I say," continued Pony, "Little Vic is just too wise for this kind of racing. What does he care about winning the money some fellow has bet on him? Some guy who hasn't even seen him maybe—just picking his name out of a newspaper. What does Little Vic care about that? But someday he's going to get into a race when it will mean something to win, and that day Little Vic *will* win."

Jack Baker pushed his hat to the back of his head and looked at Pony as if the boy had lost his mind. "Pretty soon," he said, "you'll be telling me that's what the colt just told you. This is a horse, son. He is supposed to be a race horse." He paused to glance at Little Vic. "Anyway, he still has four legs under him. He might turn into a race horse yet. Wish

81

I'd had the three thousand bucks to claim him."

Pony's eyes began to shine. "You believe in him, don't you, Mr. Baker! You feel the way I do about him!"

Jack Baker forced a smile to his lips. "Boy and man, I've been handling horses for the last forty years, and I ought to have the good sense to write this one off as a bad bargain. But, so help me, Pony, I'll be blasted if you haven't sold me on Little Vic too." He looked a long moment at the boy whose hands were smoothing the back of the horse before them. "It's sure wonderful how one fellow's faith in something can make another guy believe it too. Don't you ever say I said so, but I got a feeling that someday, somewhere, Little Vic will make good. My one hope is that you'll be there to see him do it, Pony. I sure hope so."

"Thanks, Mr. Baker," said Pony. "I'm sure going to try to be there, wherever it is, whenever it is."

He felt Jack Baker give his back a slap, but Pony didn't look around. It was good-by, and he knew it. Soon the new owner of Little Vic would be coming to claim his horse. But Pony intended to stay around to find out where Little Vic was going to be sent.

A man showed up at last, wearing a tall hat and

cowboy boots. He said his name was Joe Hills and he had orders to send Little Vic to the Harry George ranch in Arizona.

"What part of Arizona?" asked Pony.

"Southwest," said Joe Hills.

"Do you think they might need an extra hand?" asked Pony. "I've been with Little Vic since the day he was born."

Joe Hills gave him a queer look. "No," he said very quickly, "they would have no use for you a-tall."

Pony waited until he had gone off, leaving him alone with Little Vic. He wanted this good-by to be private. Very gently he lifted the colt's nose out of the feed box. The colt flung up his head and stamped a front foot. How was he to know that this friend was parting from him, perhaps for good? Pony waited, and he was glad he did. For in a moment Little Vic dropped his lovely head and began sniffing at the boy's pockets. Then he did something he had never done before. Without warning, the colt suddenly stuck his head between the boy's elbow and ribs and held it there while Pony wonderingly put his arm around it. Slowly Pony raised his other hand and scratched the colt between his ears.

"What is it, fellow?" he asked softly. "What are you trying to tell me?"

Little Vic drew his nose away and looked down into the boy's eyes. Pony, looking back, could see his own face looking out at him from the brown depths of the horse's eyes. Then Little Vic dropped his eyelids and the spell was broken. Again he turned to his feed box as if he had quite forgotten all about Pony Rivers. But the boy stepped toward the colt and laid his cheek against the warm, dark neck. He reached his hand up and gently patted the other side of the colt's neck.

"I'll be seeing you, boy," he whispered. "I'll be seeing you again, Little Vic."

Then he ran out of the stable without looking back.

Pony was now at loose ends. He had a little money, the hundred-dollar bill Lefty had given him for the fight and twenty dollars he had handed him as a parting gift. With one hundred and twenty dollars Pony could have started west in the wake of Little Vic. For a whole day he played with this idea before he decided against it. It began to seem to Pony that something more than chance had taken a hand in his future. It began to seem as if the very fact that he and Little Vic had become separated had some special meaning. All day he sat in a park under tall palm trees, looking through their slender leaves at the bright Florida sky, and tried to think of what that special meaning might be. He began to think about his father who had been a jockey. He remembered what Jack Baker had told him about learning to ride at the country fairs. And he thought about the great jockeys who had seemed to belong to certain great horses. All at once his mind was made up. He would learn to be a jockey. He was meant to be the one to ride Little Vic. That's what

Little Vic had been trying to tell him the day they parted. Now the special meaning was clear!

He sprang up from the bench, his face happy for the first time in days. He had not lost Little Vic at all! He had just learned how he could find and keep him for good! That evening Pony Rivers ate dinner in a streetcar which had been made over into an eating place. He felt so fine that he ordered chicken and ice cream. It was the first time Pony had been really hungry since the claiming race.

Now Pony had a plan, and the very next day he started to put it to work. He was able to get a job cleaning stables for one of the big owners at the track. He even took a horse out now and then in the early dawn to exercise him. But none of them got under his skin. They were just horses, good enough in their way, but not one of them, he thought, was in a class with Little Vic!

The money he picked up working around the stables Pony hung on to. He ate as little as he could get by with, and not only to save money either. Part of Pony's plan, the most important part of it, was to start riding at the country fairs during the late summer when the fairs started in the Middle West. So he wanted to

keep his weight down. He knew he could get by somehow by following the racing season in different parts
of the East and South until the fairs started. In the
meantime he would have to save enough money to
buy a riding outfit. It never entered his head that his
plan might not succeed. The same will which had sent
him from New York to the blue grass in search of
Victory, would carry him over the rough road ahead.
Though Pony would never have guessed it of himself, the one thing most necessary for success he already had in large measure. That one thing was
courage.

Pony's heart almost failed him many times during
the months before the country fairs could start. Often
he went hungry, and always he lived in fear that he
might lose his little bunch of greenbacks. He never
let anyone know how much he had, and he slept
in his clothes with his money belt safe around his
middle.

Then one hot morning in late August he found himself walking down a tree-shaded lane in the direction
of the stables at his first country fair. There were trees
everywhere, but even in the shade the heat was heavy,
and the sack over Pony's back in which he carried his

riding things had made a dark wet patch on the back of his blue shirt.

Off beyond the stables he could see a small grand-stand rising above a board fence. Following that fence around, Pony thought this track must be the smallest race track on the face of the earth. But he was to see others later even smaller than this one. Certainly it looked nothing like the tracks where the great horses ran. But Pony put a pleasant smile on his face as he approached the stables and tried not to show how little he liked the setup.

It soon became plain to Pony that there were no owners here with large stables of racers. Most of them had only one horse to their names, and that one was a family matter. Girls as well as boys were working around the stables with their fathers and mothers. They showed little interest in the newcomer, and Pony wandered slowly past them, feeling more like an outsider than he had ever felt in all his life before.

At last, down near the end of the row of stalls, he came upon an old man sitting in the shade, his back against a tree. He was holding by a long rope a dark brown, long-legged horse which looked as if once upon a time, long ago, it might have been a good race horse. Now it was old.

"Hello," said Pony to the old man.

He looked up. "Hello, son," he answered in a kindly voice. "Where did you come from?"

"East," said Pony. "I'm looking for a chance to ride."

A wise look came into the old man's eyes and he smiled slowly. "Ever done any riding?"

"No," said Pony. "That is," he added, "no racing." Then his voice took on a sudden firmness. "But I have exercised some of the best of them. All I need is a chance."

The old man looked him up and down. "You look like a jockey," he said. "Go over to the track office and give them your name and weight. If you can make one hundred and ten pounds, I think you can have this horse in the first race this afternoon."

Pony didn't look very happy at the news. The old man read his thoughts.

"I guess you don't think much of Sun Fox."

"He looks old for racing," said Pony.

The old man got slowly to his feet and pulled the

89

horse toward him. "Yes, he is old for racing. He'll be twelve in January. But a few years back he was burning up the tracks with the best of them. And he can still go for a quarter of a mile."

Pony began to feel a sudden interest in Sun Fox. He had heard about these old horses who could put on a short burst of speed.

"Ever ride a quarter horse?" asked the old man.

Pony shook his head.

"The secret of riding quarter horses is to start fast and stay in front. You got to watch for holes to break through, then slide your horse along the fence and stay there. The turns are short and dangerous. But once you get the hang of it, you can win—even with Sun Fox. The kid that was to ride him this afternoon ran out on us. I think I can talk my boss into letting you take over. That is, if you want to."

Suddenly Pony did want to. With all his heart he wanted to. Something told him that he and Sun Fox had a certain date with the future and with Little Vic. If he could only win this race, he would have other horses given him. He would be getting the experience he needed in order one day to be good enough to ride Little Vic.

Pony Has a Plan

He dropped his sack of belongings at the old man's feet. "Where's the track office?" he asked.

As soon as Pony had got all his business taken care of at the track office, he returned to the stable where the old man and Sun Fox were waiting for him.

"All fixed up?" the old man asked him. Then, "What's your name?"

Pony told him.

"Mine's Charlie," said the old man. "Charlie Pete. Just call me Charlie. I fixed it with the boss for you to ride this afternoon. He'll be dropping by later."

"I'd like to take Sun Fox around the track once to feel him out and get the lay of things," Pony told him.

"Very wise," said Charlie in his deep, quiet voice. "I'll help you saddle up."

In a few minutes Pony, looking very small on the back of the big old horse, was walking him, with Charlie at his side, toward the track.

"I wouldn't hurry him," said Charlie as they went on the track. "His wind isn't what it used to be, and he has a hard mouth. He might get the idea he wanted to race and he would use up all his steam for this afternoon."

Pony understood and held the old horse to a slow trot. As they went around the first turn, Pony began to wonder how many horses would be racing with him in a few short hours. The track was narrow, the turns short. If there was to be any rough riding, someone might take a bad spill. He hoped it would not be himself. And yet he was going to take every chance he safely could to get Sun Fox home ahead of the field—every chance possible without causing danger to his horse. Pony didn't worry so much about hurting himself.

"Good old Sun Fox," he said and leaned forward to pat the old racer's neck.

That afternoon, with the grandstand filled with farmers and their wives and children, Pony weighed in at the judges' stand and got up on Sun Fox. There was no real parade to the post. No man in a bright red coat on a fine-looking gray pony led the way to the starting gate. These horses needed no careful handling. Most of them were old, and all of them were family pets. They had no bad streaks and not enough spirit to be on edge. The other six riders were either boys like Pony who were trying to get a start as jockeys, or else the sons of farmers and racing their own horses. But they all knew one another and they treated Pony like an outsider.

The winner's money for this race was fifty dollars. If Pony won, he would receive one tenth of that, or five dollars. It would be enough to keep him in food for a few days, and he could sleep somewhere around the stables.

The horses lined up quietly at the starting gate and in a moment they were off.

Pony had only one thought, and that was to get Sun Fox started ahead of the others and get him to the fence where he could save distance. The moment he felt the old racer's big body bunch under him for that first wild leap, Pony flung himself forward on his horse's neck and yelled to him. Sun Fox pounded forward a little ahead of the others. Pony could see bobbing noses on either side of him, and he urged Sun Fox to greater speed. The wind whistled past his ears, but he couldn't feel the horse's feet landing under him. It seemed as if he were flying, and a smile split his face. The old racer could go! But could he keep it up? Now they were coming into the turn. Pony let his eyes slide toward the fence. Another rider with the same idea as Pony was whipping his horse into the turn. Pony laid his own whip very lightly against Sun Fox's side to let the old fellow know he was still in a race. Then timing his next move to a split second, Pony guided his horse to the fence. But Sun Fox needed no guiding! The old horse had a lot more experience than his rider. He put on a burst of speed and as smoothly as a shadow eased himself across in front of the others without ever crowding one of them. Now he was on the fence and well in front of the field. Pony yelled into his ears and Sun Fox held his lead. They flashed past the grandstand with a bay colt coming up fast to Sun Fox's neck. But as if he knew that every inch counted, the old racer stuck his head out and hung on gamely, and it was Sun Fox's race by a nose.

Charlie, along with Sun Fox's owner, was waiting at the gate as Pony rode off the track. It was something of a shock to the boy to discover that there was no winner's circle at this track. It would have been great fun to ride Sun Fox into the circle and to watch the admiring faces of the crowd as the newsmen gathered round to take pictures. Then right in the middle of his dreaming, Pony was forced to remember that, had this been one of those tracks, neither he nor

Sun Fox would have been on it. Besides, he wanted to save the winner's circle for Little Vic. So he accepted with thanks the good wishes of the owner and Charlie, and pocketed his five dollars.

Pony did get other horses after that race on Sun Fox. He didn't win every time. But he won often enough to send him on his way at last with some added money in his pocket and the right to call himself a jockey.

7. West

I<small>T WAS</small> getting on into October. Pony's luck had held. He had worked his way west, gathering good experience and no small sum of money as he traveled. The money belt had more of its pockets filled than when he had started out. It was true that none of the bills in it were hundred-dollar bills, like that one Lefty had given him. But there were enough smaller ones

96

to make a fair-sized nest egg, and Pony continued to hang on to every cent he could.

He wandered onto a race track one day where the fair had been over for a week but where the racing continued because the weather had held and the grandstands were filled every afternoon. Pony entered his name on the track records, and his good riding soon made him a favorite rider among the owners and the crowds.

But the other jockeys didn't like Pony. One reason for this was because he won too many times. Most of them were farm boys and they had not had the experience at racing that Pony had gained this summer.

One day as he rode his horse toward the starting gate Pony had a queer feeling inside his bones that all was not going to be well with him. He longed for the race to start in order that it could be over. He intended to leave this place this very day. It was the first time in his life that Pony had ever had the feeling that people around him didn't like him. And the worst of the feeling was that they didn't dislike him for any harm he had ever done to them; they simply didn't like him for what he was. All in all, Pony was a very unhappy boy as the horses took their places in the starting gate.

As soon as the race began, Pony understood that he was in for a bad time. The other riders seemed to be less interested in winning the race than in keeping Pony from winning. They blocked him from the start, and one boy, reaching out, even struck Pony's horse in the head with his whip. The horse jumped to one side, striking another which had come up to crowd him. In the next moment they were at the turn with the two horses so wild with fear they were all but impossible to handle. Then it happened. Not even Pony, who was on his guard, could have told how it happened. His horse was forced into the fence. He had just time to know that his horse was falling when all the world went black.

By the time Pony came to, a couple of days later, his world was a greatly changed one. He had no idea how much time had gone by since the fall. When he first looked around him he rather expected to find himself lying on the track with the blue sky over his head and perhaps a horse with a broken shoulder lying somewhere near him.

Instead, what Pony saw was the foot of a bed. There

was a snow-white cover on the bed. And lifted up in front of him by a rope, was a large, white bundle of something which Pony soon discovered was his right leg. He looked to one side of him, but it was hard to turn his head because of the strange cap he was wearing. He tried to raise his right arm to feel that head covering, and then he found that his right arm would not move and was done up in as big a bundle as his leg.

On either side of him he saw beds stretching away to the walls. Pony closed his eyes, suddenly very tired. He tried to take in what had happened. Oh, yes, there had been a fall, and so now here he was in bed.

He thought he had gone to sleep again when he heard a voice say very softly, "Can you open your eyes today?"

Pony opened his eyes at once and looked up into the face of a woman. She had white hair and a white cap and a white dress on. Pony thought she was the whitest person he had ever seen. But her hand against his cheek was cool, and for a moment he wondered if the white lady could be made of snow. He knew, of course, that she couldn't really be, but he felt all mixed up in his mind.

"Can you talk?" asked the lady.

"Yes," said Pony in a whisper.

"Not that you haven't been talking a great deal of the time since you came in here," went on the lady. She was busy with something on the table beside Pony's bed. "You have been calling for your little brother. Do you remember that?" She looked down at him and smiled.

Pony felt more mixed up than ever. I have no little brother, he thought, and didn't know that he had spoken the words out loud.

"That's funny," said the lady still in the same pleasant voice that seemed somehow cool, like her hands. "If you don't have a little brother, then who is Little Vic?"

So that was it! He had been calling Little Vic's name. And they had thought Little Vic was his brother! Suddenly Pony smiled. Little Vic his brother! Then the smile went away, and what showed of Pony's face was drawn up in deep thought. Come to think of it, Little Vic *was* a kind of brother to him. He was the one thing on earth he loved the most and wanted the most. Could you be the brother of a horse? No, certainly not, Pony told himself, and shook his head.

A small cry burst from him. It hurt to move his head quickly.

The lady leaned over him again.

"My head," said Pony.

"I know," she said. "You had a bad fall and you have hurt your head. You must lie very still for many days yet."

"When can I get up?" asked Pony. He didn't really want to get up at all right now. But it would help to know how long he would have to stay here.

"Not for a long time," said the lady. "Not for many weeks. But try not to feel bad about it. You're a very lucky boy to be alive."

"What happened to the horse?" asked Pony. "Did they have to kill him?"

"The horse?" she asked in some surprise. "How on earth should I know what happened to the horse? Now don't talk any more. Take this." She placed a pill on his tongue and gave him a sip of water. "You must go to sleep again."

The weeks went by somehow. Pony lost all track of time. More than two full months had rolled off the year before he was allowed to go on his way again. His bones had mended perfectly, so Pony knew some of his luck still held. But all of his money had gone to pay his bills. And the worst thing that could happen to a jockey had happened to Pony. The blow on his head had done something to him. He was afraid to ride again!

When he thought of the racing he had done he would shake all over. How had he ever had the courage to climb on a horse? he asked himself. He tried to think of exercising Little Vic and of the gay glad rides they had often had together in the early dawn. But it was no use. It hurt him to have to own up to it, even to himself, but the simple truth remained—he would be afraid to ride Little Vic if Little Vic were standing in front of him. He visited stables and tried working around horses again, thinking he could throw off his fear. But it didn't work. He was through as a jockey. He would never ride Little Vic again.

Still Pony knew that he wanted to find the horse. There was nothing in life for him now but to find Little Vic. Even though he never sat his back again, he could still be near him, loving him and caring for him. So, working when he could, getting lifts whenever the chance came along, Pony continued to turn his steps toward Arizona.

West

One day in January, Honey Green looked out of the kitchen window of the Harry George ranchhouse and saw a stranger coming up the road from the highway. He looked very small against the wide Arizona country, and he walked like one who was very tired, and he carried a sack on his back. Honey knew from experience that every newcomer to the ranch found the kitchen door sooner or later. So she went on with her baking, only looking up now and then to watch the stranger's approach.

At last Honey's eyes widened and her busy brown hands lay quiet on the edge of her mixing bowl. "For the love of goodness," she said. "Now what do you suppose *he* wants here?" There was no one around to answer her question, but Honey did not have long to wait for an answer. There came a gentle knock on the back door and she hurried to open it.

Pony had somehow got the idea in his head that the first person he would meet at the Harry George ranch would be Joe Hills. He didn't remember exactly what the man looked like, but at least he was a man. It was therefore a little surprising for Pony to find himself looking up into the face of a little skinny woman the color of an old penny and with hair the same color growing close to her head in very tight little waves. Somehow he had never thought of a woman, any kind of a woman at all, being a part of the Harry George outfit.

"What do you want, child?" said Honey quickly but not unkindly.

"I'm looking for Little Vic," said Pony, then sat down on the doorstep because he didn't have the strength to stand on his feet any longer.

"Seems to me like you ought to have something to eat before you go about looking for anybody," declared Honey. "Come into the kitchen. I just took the bread out a moment ago and there is all the milk you can drink."

Pony rose slowly and followed her. When he had swallowed a glass of milk and a large piece of bread with jam and butter on it, Honey said, "Now who is this Little Vic you came here to see?"

Pony looked at her in surprise. "You mean you never heard of him?" he asked. Then a new fear came over him. "Isn't Little Vic here? Have they sold him?"

"You have to tell me who he is before I can tell you much about him." Honey moved over to the sink and began to run water into her baking dishes.

"He's a horse," said Pony. "One of the best horses that ever lived."

"Oh," said Honey without turning around, "then he's down at the stables with all the others. All they think about around here is horses. Just horses, horses, horses. Seems to me some people are plain foolish about horses. Like Mr. and Mrs. George. They are out in California right this very minute with some they took to race there. If it's a horse you want to see, just go down to the stables and take your pick. Me, I don't want any part of them."

Pony thanked her for the food and went out of the house. He had no trouble finding the stables. And once there he had no trouble finding Little Vic. He was standing in his box stall, his head over the half-door. Pony would have known that head among a thousand.

"Little Vic," he called. "Little Vic, boy. Remember me?"

The horse turned his head as Pony's voice reached him. His ears pointed toward the boy, and his nose widened as he sent a soft greeting to the friend now running toward him. Pony took Little Vic's head in his arms and laid his cheek against the horse's forelock.

For a moment he could say nothing at all, but ran his fingers over Little Vic's neck and between his ears. Then, "You remembered me," he said over and over again. "You remembered me, Little Vic."

He opened the stall and went inside. He felt down the horse's legs and, as always, Little Vic showed how little he liked this kind of thing. Pony smiled. It was like old times again. It didn't matter now that he had lost his heart for racing. Nothing mattered at all except that here he was beside Little Vic at last.

A voice cut across his happiness. "What are you doing with that horse?"

Pony straightened up and looked into the cold blue eyes of Joe Hills.

"He remembers me," said Pony to the man, not knowing him at first.

"Then he's one up on me," said the man. "As far as I can tell I never saw you before." His face darkened. "Get out of that stall."

Pony laughed. Now he remembered the man. He was Joe Hills, and he found it funny that Mr. Hills should be ordering him out of Little Vic's stall.

"I remember you now, Mr. Hills," he said. "I was the boy who took care of this colt from the time he was born. I'm Pony Rivers. I was there when you took Little Vic away after the claiming race."

"What are you doing here?"

"Nothing, I guess," said Pony. "I been riding all this past summer, but I came west just to be near Little Vic. We sort of belong together." He laughed again. "Why, when I was hurt I even got to thinking that me and him were brothers."

But Joe Hills didn't return the laugh, although a smile came to his face. It was not, however, the kind of smile that made you want to smile with him. As Pony looked at it, a strange fear came into his heart.

"Well," began Joe Hills slowly, "you *are* about the same color, for a fact." A mean look came into his face. "We don't want no colored riders around here. As I see it, there isn't no such thing as a colored jockey. And I don't even want no colored exercise boys on this place. We might be able to use you around the stables. But you can't never ride this horse or any other. Understand?"

Pony understood all too well. Joe Hills was like those boys who had caused his fall so many months ago. They had not liked him because he was colored. And now Joe Hills didn't want him to ride for the same reason. It made no sense at all to Pony. It only made him feel sick inside.

Joe Hills went away, and Pony came out of Little Vic's stall. He stood looking at the horse and thinking things over. At least Joe Hills had not told him to go. And Pony didn't really want to ride anyway. Or did he? He leaned across the half-door to lay his hand on Little Vic's silky back. Would he be afraid on Little Vic? Would he?

For the next week Pony made himself useful around the ranch. He tried to keep out of Joe Hills' way as much as possible. And he tried to stay as close to Little Vic as he could. The horse was a three-year-old now and looked better than he ever had. Could he run, Pony asked himself? Would he run? He tried to find out from the other fellows working around the stables. But they thought very little of this son of Victory. He had shown nothing in his workouts so far to make them think that he was anything special. Mr. George had not bothered to take him to Santa Anita. The feeling among the men seemed to be that this time the boss had got stung.

Honey Green was Pony's best friend at the ranch. Without her, Pony would have been a lonely boy in-

deed. Because of the way Joe Hills had acted, Pony
stayed away from all the men as much as he could.
He was therefore glad of Honey's friendly feeling
toward him. Even though she did not have any interest in horses, they still had something in common, these
two. They belonged to the same race.

Often at the end of the day Honey and Pony would
be alone in the kitchen. She asked him a lot of ques-
tions about his past while he helped her with the dishes.

"Didn't you ever go to school?" she wanted to
know one evening.

"Sure," said Pony, "all I needed to. I finished all
eight grades. I can read and write, and what I know
about horses would take years to find out at school.
And where is the school that could teach me?"

"Maybe that's true," she said, "but it don't seem
right for a boy your age to be knocking around the
country not learning anything."

"But I *am* learning something, Honey," he said. "I'm
learning something every day. Look at all the country
I've seen. Look what I've learned about people. What
difference does it make whether you learn it at school
or on your own? And I know all the school stuff I
need to be a stable boy."

"All the same," declared Honey, "your mother would have made you do different if she had lived." She grew thoughtful for a moment, then said, "Seems like I ought to do something about it just because she would have wanted it." Suddenly she turned to Pony. "If you are going to stay around here, you are going to get some teaching for the good of your soul. It won't hurt me none, either. Every night from now on, you and I are going to read something from the Good Book together. If it don't do nothing else for you, it will help you to bear with fellows like Joe Hills."

Pony had learned by now that when Honey made up her mind about anything there was no use trying to change it. So now he held his tongue, for it was plain that Honey *had* made up her mind.

She decided to begin with the Book of Job. "He had a lot of things to put up with too," she told Pony, "and his faith in the goodness of God gave him the strength to bear with every one of them. People like us need a lot of faith to bear some of the things we got to." She fixed him with her eye. "And faith in something besides horses," she added as she pushed a pair of glasses onto her broad nose.

"Yes, ma'am," said Pony in a small voice.

Pony had thought that the Book of Job would have very little interest for him, and the first part of it proved him right. And then one night Honey began to read something that made Pony raise his head and listen with his heart in his eyes.

" 'Hast thou given the horse strength?' " Honey read. " 'Hast thou clothed his neck with thunder? Canst thou make him afraid as a grasshopper? The glory of his nostrils is terrible. He paweth in the valley, and rejoiceth in his strength. He goeth on to meet the armed men.' "

When Honey had finished that part Pony asked her to read it over to him again, and repeated the words softly to himself when she had finished, "Hast thou clothed his neck with thunder?" Was Little Vic that kind of horse? Pony was so lost in his wondering that he didn't hear the sniff with which Honey closed the Bible and put it back on its shelf among Mrs. George's cookbooks.

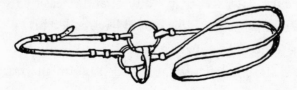

8. With Thunder on His Neck

As the days went by Pony found it easy to settle into what Joe Hills would have called his "place" at the ranch. As a matter of fact, Pony's life here was little different from what it had been on the farm in the blue grass where Little Vic was born. His duties were about the same. And yet, though his life seemed little different, he felt entirely different inside himself. A shadow had been cast over his happiness by Joe Hills. Pony knew that he could never be really happy here as long as Joe Hills felt about him the way he did. However, there was Little Vic, and Pony was quite sure that he would rather take the Joe Hills kind of unhappiness than the sorrow he would feel if he had to be separated from the horse again. So he tried to do his work as well as he could, and he kept out of sight of Joe Hills as much as possible.

At first he had tried to be content just taking care of the horse. But the longer he was around Little Vic, the more Pony began to wonder if he would ever have the courage to ride him if the chance were given him. The more he thought about it, the more he wondered. And the more he wondered, the more it seemed to him that he would never be at peace until he had put himself to the test.

One evening he made an excuse to Honey and disappeared into the night as soon as the dishes were done. The moon was coming up above the rim of mountains to the east. Off to the west there were banks of clouds in the sky. There had been heavy rains in those mountains a short time ago. Honey had warned him about the storm before he had gone out into the night.

"If you plan to go wandering around by yourself," she had told him, "you be mighty careful to stay out of the draw."

"Why?" Pony had asked.

The draw was a dry riverbed and looked like a big crack in the earth. It ran for some miles along the highway until it joined a wide and shallow river to the east.

"What's wrong with the draw?" Pony had wanted to know.

"Isn't anything wrong with the draw. The good Lord put it there for a good purpose. It carries off the flood water that comes running down off the mountains. That water comes down faster than a train of cars when there has been a big storm in the mountains, like today. Sometimes folks that don't know any better get caught in the flood and drown before they can say scat."

"I'll keep out of the draw," Pony had promised her. It made him feel good to know that Honey was interested in his safety. It made him feel as if he had found a real friend at last.

But Pony had not planned to go into the draw. This was the night he had decided to find out if he had the courage to ride Little Vic. He would have to be very careful, because Joe Hills had told him never to ride the horse. Until now it had been easy to obey that rule. Now, however, Pony knew that he must try to ride Little Vic. If he didn't have the courage to run him, then he could settle down forever, glad just to be the horse's stable boy. But the idea would not die in Pony that perhaps he and the horse were meant to race together. If they were, then he would have the courage to race him. Tonight was going to prove to him once and for all which it should be— jockey or stable boy.

The desert floor was white under the moonlight when Pony approached the stables. As he went past the house where the ranch hands slept, Pony looked in the windows and saw Joe Hills sitting at a table with four other men. They were playing cards, and they looked as if they would be sitting there for many hours to come.

Pony went first to the tack room where he had put

his riding things. Then he went to Little Vic's stall and saddled up. He led the horse out and closed the stall door very carefully behind him. Then, still leading the horse, Pony started across the open fields toward the highway. As always, Little Vic went quietly along. Pony knew now that he would have no fear of riding him at a walk. He had the courage to get on. But he had first to find something to stand on in order to get into the saddle. The irons were high up on the horse's side, the way jockeys always have them, and Pony's legs were too short to make the long reach from the ground to where the irons hung.

After walking about half a mile without finding either a tree stump or a rock large enough to be of any use, Pony decided to try to get the horse close enough to the wire fence to let him stand on one of the posts and make a jump for the saddle. It took some time to get Little Vic close to the fence, and an even longer time to get him to stand still long enough for Pony to get into the saddle. Little Vic was not used to this kind of thing. And all the while Pony's footing on the post was anything but sure. At last, however, he was sitting on the horse's back, very happy to be there after the

struggle. Pony did not realize that in his efforts to get
on his horse he had quite forgotten to be afraid.

He guided the horse at a walk a little distance off
the highway in the direction of the western mountains.
He found it good to be riding again, even at a walk. A
smile appeared on Pony's face and stayed there. Suppose he and Little Vic just disappeared into the wide
land out beyond. Suppose he just kept on riding west.
It was a lovely idea, and for a moment Pony played
with it. He was sure the horse would be happier with
him than with Joe Hills. Perhaps even more than
with Harry George, who, for all Pony knew, might
be just like Joe Hills. But then Little Vic belonged to
Harry George, so that settled that.

Little Vic's long legs carried him over the ground
at a good clip even at a walk. His steps were wide apart,
and he held his head high and looked about him as he
went. Pony dared at last to lift himself in the saddle,
and Little Vic began to trot. After a bit Pony pulled
him up. It had been all right! He had not been afraid.
If only he had the strength of mind to let Little Vic
run. But no matter how Pony talked to himself, he
couldn't bring himself to the point of letting Vic
really go.

They were riding along the edge of the draw now. The ground was hard and even. The draw itself was a deep shadow in the moonlight, splitting the desert floor in two.

Suddenly Pony was surprised to see a light up ahead of him. It was an unsteady light and seemed to come from the very bottom of the draw. He moved Little Vic into a trot, and before long came up to where some people had settled themselves around a campfire in the bottom of the draw.

Pony drew up Little Vic and called down to them, "You had better not try to camp there."

Now they saw him sitting his horse just above their heads.

"Why not?" one of the men called out, and a woman laughed.

"It's not safe," Pony told him. "There have been heavy rains in the mountains today, and a flash flood might come down this draw and drown you in your sleep."

The man laughed. "Do you expect us to believe that?"

"It's the truth," said Pony.

"You people out West are always telling tall tales

to newcomers," said the man. "But you can't fool us with that one."

"Besides," called up another woman, "if the wind should come up we will be out of it down here. It's a lovely place to camp."

Pony saw that he could not change their plan, so he said no more but trotted Little Vic on past them and their car, which was parked off the highway at a little distance from them.

"Maybe Honey didn't have the right of it," he said aloud to Little Vic. He laughed at himself. "Maybe like the man said, she was just telling me a story because I'm new to the country too. Maybe she was a little mad at me for not staying in for the reading tonight."

Pony thought he had ridden something over a mile when suddenly Little Vic began to act jumpy. His ears pointed stiffly forward and he slowed his pace as if he were listening for something. Suddenly he stopped altogether, and Pony could feel his body shaking slightly under the saddle. Little Vic, for the first time since he was a very young colt, was afraid! Pony peered into the shadowy spaces out before him. He listened with all his might. And after a moment or two he thought he heard the roar of thunder. Little Vic had begun to dance from side to side and to toss his head. Pony tried to talk to him, remembering that horses are often afraid of thunder. But Little Vic would not be quieted. He began to paw at the ground. And now Pony heard what Little Vic had heard at the start. That roar was not thunder. It was the sound of racing water rolling down from the mountains with all the force of its quick drop to the valley floor behind it. Pony waited only an instant before he turned Little Vic and began trotting back the way they had come. The horse was nearly wild now. He fought the bit and shook his head. Little Vic wanted to run. And then in a flash the whole world seemed to be caught up in one great roar as the water came racing toward them. How could such a flood come so fast, where only moments ago there had been a dry river-bed? No wonder they called them flash floods, Pony thought. And in the next instant he remembered the people camping in the draw. At the speed the water was coming, they could never get away in time. They might even be asleep by now and would never know about their danger until it was too late to do anything about it.

With Thunder on His Neck

Thinking of those people, Pony quite forgot that he had been afraid ever to race again. He leaned forward over Little Vic's neck. Old habit was acting for him now, and without knowing that he did so, he gathered his horse for the start exactly as if he were in the stall of a starting gate. Then he gave the yell which had sent many a quarter horse leaping out ahead of the field and down the track and away. Little Vic needed no other urging. With a powerful spring he was off, and Pony's heart leaped with him. Now he remembered his old fear, but he was no longer afraid. This was the moment he had lived for ever since the first moment he had looked upon Little Vic. He knew that now. They had both been waiting for this moment because they had been meant for each other from the start.

Suddenly he began to talk to the horse, his small body bunched upon the horse's neck.

"This is the race you've been waiting for, fellow. This is the real thing. There isn't any money riding on you today. But the prize is the biggest one you'll ever win. It's the lives of all those people, Little Vic. If you aren't as good as I think you are, they won't have a chance. But you are. *You are!*"

The last two words were a yell. For Little Vic had settled into his speed. No, not his speed, after all. Only one horse had ever set such a pace in any race anywhere. That horse was Victory. But he had never raced for such a cause as this. He could be proud of this son.

The roar was coming closer. Pony looked back once, as he might have done in a regular race to see how close the nearest horse was to him. But he could see nothing but the shadowy draw, and he began to wonder whether the sound he heard was the thunder of Little Vic's galloping feet or the sound of the flood.

He tried to remember the distance they had come. Was it a mile? Was it two miles? Could Little Vic, could *any* horse, keep this pace for a mile? Now another yell burst from Pony as he realized that they had drawn away from the sound of the water. Little Vic had gained! He might yet outrace the flood. Long legs were moving smoothly, strongly under him, never slowing in their pace, like a machine that could go on and on forever. But Pony knew that no horse could keep this pace for long. He drew him up a little, saving him for the stretch. In a moment the sound of the water again came to his ears.

With Thunder on His Neck

All at once Pony caught sight of a small dot of light out ahead of them. The campfire. This was the stretch. He touched Little Vic with his whip and the horse flew over the ground. As they came up to the fire Pony fought to stop him. "Get out," he screamed to the campers. "The flood. It's coming! Don't stop for anything. Just get out!"

The astonished campers hardly believed him at first. Then they too caught the sound of the approaching thunder. Without waiting longer, they began to climb the bank of the draw, and they barely had time to get their breath before the flood had rolled over their campfire and swept their belongings away.

Now, at last, Little Vic stood in a winner's circle as the people he had saved closed round him in admiring wonder.

"He raced the flood and won," Pony told them simply. "There was no one to see, but he ran the greatest race of them all."

Like a great winner, Little Vic stood with head high, looking out past the people. In the moonlight his brown coat shone and the whites of his eyes flashed. Pony smiled and laid his hand upon the horse's neck. He was remembering something Honey had read to him a few nights back as he said, "There won't be a horseshoe of roses to slip over your head, fellow. Not for this race. But it isn't every horse that has a neck that's clothed with thunder. That's you, Little Vic. A horse with thunder on his neck."

9. Pony Meets a Horseman

Pony was cooling out Little Vic in front of the stables when Joe Hills found him. Pony had known he would be found out, but it never entered his head to put the horse in his stall without first cooling him out. And Pony didn't greatly care if Joe Hills did find him. Just now nothing mattered except Little Vic's greatness. With that to warm his heart, Pony could take whatever punishment Joe Hills might plan for him. Even if he were sent away from the ranch, as he expected he would be, it would not be for long. Now that he and the horse had proved they belonged together, nothing would keep them apart for long.

"Some people drove in a little while ago with a story about a horse that saved them from a flash flood. What do you know about it?"

Pony stopped walking Little Vic around to look at the angry man before him. "It's the truth," he said. "Little Vic ran the greatest race of all time. You should have seen him, Mr. Hills. He never took a wrong step. He was great."

Joe Hills walked up to Pony as if he intended to hit him, and the boy stepped back.

"I told you never to ride that horse or any other on the ranch," said Joe Hills. "Now you get off this place. This minute. Right now."

"After I finish cooling out Little Vic," said Pony.

"After nothing," roared Joe Hills. "You think you can take three thousand dollars' worth of horse out and run him in the moonlight and give me cheek besides? For two cents I'd knock your block off!"

"He saved their lives," said Pony, walking Little Vic again.

Pony Meets a Horseman

"What do I care about their lives?" yelled Joe Hills. "They were dumb enough to camp in the draw—that was their lookout. But suppose something happened to the horse? Did you ever stop to think about that?" There followed a long account of what Joe Hills thought of Pony Rivers, and none of it contained a word of praise. "There ought to be some way of putting you in jail," he finished.

He grabbed the lead rope from Pony's hands, giving the boy a hard push. Pony walked away, looking back once at the man and horse going around and around in a wide circle. Pony hoped Joe Hills would not take out his anger on Little Vic.

Pony went at once to the tack room and got his riding things and put them in the sack in which he had carried them here. Then he went up to the ranchhouse to say good-by to Honey.

"You know you had no business taking that horse, Pony," she told him. "Mr. George would be as mad at you as Joe is if he knew."

Pony looked unhappily at her. "Do you think he really would? Is he that kind of a fellow?"

Honey sighed. "He's a good man, but he sets a lot of store by his horses. He would not like to think that every Tom, Dick, and Harry was running them in the dark."

"It wasn't dark, Honey. The moon was bright as day. That is why I chose tonight. I'm the only person in the world that can race Little Vic. He knows it, and so do I." Pony paused for a minute. "And I am going to try and make Mr. George believe it too."

"What you planning to do?" asked Honey.

"I'm going to Santa Anita and find Mr. George, and I'm going to tell him about Little Vic's race. Maybe I can make him see it the way it is. Maybe I can make him understand."

Honey said nothing for a minute. She stood in the middle of the kitchen, looking hard at the floor, as if she were in deep thought. Then she crossed over to the bread box. "You'll need a lunch," she declared "It's a long way to Santa Anita. You'll be days getting there—if you get there at all."

She fixed him food enough for several lunches, and Pony thanked her. Then he swung his sack onto his shoulder and started once more into the west. The moonlight made the highway pavement a white ribbon stretching endlessly in front of him. Now and then the headlights of a speeding automobile made the moonlight seem less bright. Whenever a car came along which was going in his direction, Pony thumbed it as a matter of course. But he had little hope of being picked up in the night in this lonesome land. And he wasn't. After walking several miles he turned off the road. Using his sack for a pillow, he fell asleep.

The next morning the bright desert sun woke Pony. He ate one of Honey's sandwiches and started again up the highway. After a while a truck came along. Pony thumbed it, as usual, and was pleasantly surprised when it slowed down and stopped. He ran to catch up with it.

"Where you going?" the driver called down from the cab to the boy on the edge of the highway.

"California," said Pony, then added, "Santa Anita."

"You a jockey?" asked the truck driver, his eyes taking note of Pony's small figure.

Pony nodded.

"What you got in that sack?"

Pony spilled its contents onto the highway. "This is food," he explained, holding up Honey's bundle.

"Okay," said the man. "Guess I'm not taking much of a chance on a fellow with your build and packing a saddle on his back." Pony climbed into the cab and the driver started the truck. He turned with a smile toward Pony. "Gets mighty lonesome traveling through this kind of country," he said.

Two days later Pony walked through the gates of the great Santa Anita race track. He thought it just about the most beautiful place he had ever seen, with the mountains rising so close and the flowers blooming wherever he looked. It was early morning and the place seemed empty. But Pony knew that wherever the stables were he would find plenty of people and plenty of stir and action.

When he finally came to the stable area he found himself stopped by a guard at the gate. It was something new for Pony to find himself forbidden to go to the stables at a race track.

"I'm looking for Mr. Harry George," he told the guard. "He's racing some horses here."

The guard checked. "That's right," he said firmly. "You got a pass?"

No, Pony didn't have a pass.

"Can't let you in without a pass," said the guard. He waved Pony to one side in order to look at the passes of others who were going in through the gate. Pony watched them and tried to think that some morning soon maybe he would be walking through that gate too. Just beyond him was the track, and already horses with their exercise boys in the saddle were being taken out for their morning workouts. Would he ever be riding Little Vic in the early morning along this track? Pony asked himself.

It was good to be near a track again, even if he was not allowed to go to the stables. Just standing here, he could see the horses. He could spot the jockeys as they showed their passes to the guard and walked through to where their horses were waiting for them. He could smell the good sharp smell of the stables as the morning wind brought it to him.

All morning he hung around in the neighborhood of the stables. But with the approach of post time he took himself over to the grandstand and waited near the entrance to the box seats. Pony knew that all owners had box seats. The man taking the tickets had promised Pony that he would let him know when Harry George came along.

Just before post time the ticket man called, "Hey, kid," and Pony dashed over to him. "Here comes George now. The tall fellow."

Pony saw a tall thin man coming slowly toward him

surrounded by a party of men and women. He was so tanned by strong sunlight that his face was almost as dark as Pony's. When he was just about to go in through the little gate, Pony found the courage to speak.

"Mr. George. Mr. Harry George," he said.

The man turned without surprise and looked down at Pony. "Are you calling me?" he asked.

Pony swallowed. "I just came from the ranch, Mr. George, and I came to tell you about Little Vic."

Mr. George's face showed how much Pony's words troubled him. He told the others to go on, then he stepped closer to Pony. "What about Little Vic?" he asked.

Pony took a deep breath and sailed into his story. He knew he would have to tell it fast. And he knew he would have to tell it in such a way that this stranger would believe him. What Pony didn't know was that anyone looking into his eyes, so deep and troubled and honest, could never think he would tell anything but the truth.

"Three nights ago I took Little Vic out along the draw and a flash flood came up and he raced it back to where some people were camped and he won."

Pony Meets a Horseman

That took all of Pony's breath to tell, and he had to take three more quick ones before he could go on. But Harry George waited, never taking his eyes off Pony's face. Then Pony went on, his voice rising as his excitement grew in the telling. "He *is* great, Mr. George. Really great. I've known him ever since he was born, and I say he's great. But he won't run for anyone but me. I know. I've seen him. With me on him, he could win the Handicap. Honest, Mr. George."

Mr. George was not interested at the moment in Little Vic's chances in the Handicap. "What was Joe Hills thinking of to let you run that horse in the dark along the draw?" His voice was hard and low.

"Oh, he didn't let me," Pony explained quickly. "He told me never to ride him. But I had to. I just had to, Mr. George. That horse is like my own brother. I had to find out if I could ride him because I'd lost my nerve. And I had to find out if he would give me more than he had ever given anybody else."

"And did he?" asked Harry George, his voice less angry now.

"He gave me the heart out of his body," said Pony.

Mr. George smiled. It was the first time he had, and Pony's lifted face drank in that smile like a sunflower meeting the first warm rays of the day.

"I don't have a horse until the third race," said the man. "Suppose we sit down here and you tell me what this is all about."

"Yes, sir," said Pony. "That is what I came out here for. To find you and tell you all about it."

By the time the third race was called, Harry George had heard such a story of faith and love as seldom happens even in the life of a horse lover. That this boy should have risked hardship and actual suffering in order to prove a horse's greatness made Harry George decide to give Pony a break. Pony had said he was a jockey. Well, the man would let him prove it.

"I'll meet you at the stables tomorrow morning, Pony," he said. He reached into his pocket and took out a roll of bills. He peeled off a couple and handed them to Pony. "Go over to the office and put your name down as a jockey. If you can make the weight, and if you can ride, I may have a horse for you tomorrow afternoon. Keep the change for yourself. See you at six."

It was a very happy Pony who presented himself at the stable gate before six the next morning. The same guard was on duty.

Pony Meets a Horseman

"You got a pass?" he asked.

Pony smiled this time. "Mr. George said there would be one here for me. The name is Pony Rivers."

The guard checked. "Okay," he called, and Pony walked inside.

He was early for Mr. George, as he had intended to be. He wanted to get a look at the horses before the owner showed up. They looked pretty good, he decided, but of course nowhere near as good as Little Vic. Still, they were far ahead of the horses he had ridden last fall.

When Mr. George arrived he told Pony to get onto a tall, thin horse. He was not a pretty animal, but Mr. George had decided to run him this afternoon in the hope of rain. Sun Alarm, as the horse was called, liked to run in the mud, and he had been saved for that purpose.

Mr. George got on a pony and, with Pony Rivers riding beside him, started for the track. It struck Pony suddenly that he had never before known an owner like Mr. George. He had liked him from the start, but now a new feeling was entering his heart for the man. That feeling was respect. Here was no rich man who kept a string of horses as a kind of plaything.

Little Vic

Here was no betting man who looked upon a horse as an easy way to make a lot of money—maybe. Here was a man who knew horses and who loved them. He was the very man to be Little Vic's owner.

"Take him around easy once to warm him up," Mr. George was saying. "When I give you the signal, let him run. I'll time you for the quarter mile."

Had there really been a time when he had been afraid to race? Pony asked himself. It seemed impossible to believe that now, as he went carefully around the white-fenced track exactly as Mr. George had ordered him to go. Other horses went past him, their exercise boys singing as they galloped easily by. The giant mountains still had shadows down their sides, but the day was growing bright above the rims. The sky, however, was overcast. There would be rain soon. In an hour the workouts would be over for the day and the horses in their stalls waiting for the first race to be called. If it had not been for Little Vic, Pony told himself, he would have missed all this and all that lay ahead. It was Little Vic who had drawn him to the West and shown him how to race again.

At Mr. George's signal, Pony sent his horse flying down the track in a sudden burst of speed. His training at the country races had taught him how to get a horse away to a good start. At the quarter pole he pulled up and finished the distance at a trot.

"You can ride, all right, Pony," said Mr. George with a friendly smile. "Think you want to take him on this afternoon?" He looked up at the sky, then back to Pony. "There will be mud. You'll have to eat a lot of it."

"I can take it if Sun Alarm can," declared the boy.

That afternoon the fans in the grandstand watched a rather dull race. Neither the winning horse nor his rider was known to the crowd, and a very sloppy track had put most of the betting off. It was of little importance to anyone watching it that a horse named Sun Alarm, owner Harry George, rider Pony Rivers, won the fifth race. The jockey was a "bug boy" too. He had not yet ridden a year. Just luck that he should have got hold of a good "mudder."

But to that bug boy, sitting his horse in the winner's circle, there were rainbows all around the track. He couldn't wipe the smile off his face as he saw the newsmen gathering round, their cameras aimed in his direction. And he was too happy to notice the mud which the horses' feet had thrown on his face.

Harry George reached up and took Pony's hand. "There's one thing sure, Pony," he said, smiling slowly. "None of that mud you're wearing on your face is going to show up in the pictures. They're going to turn out just swell."

Pony laughed and squeezed Mr. George's hand hard.

"As soon as the eighth race is over," said Mr. George, "you and I must plan how we're going to get Little Vic up here for the Handicap"

Pony sucked in his breath. "You mean it, Mr. George?"

"If he can run the way you think he can," said Little Vic's owner. "I'll enter him in the 'Cap with one Pony Rivers up. We've got about three weeks to get him ready. Think we can do it?"

Pony's face was dead serious as he replied, "He's ready now, Mr. George. He can take any of them right now."

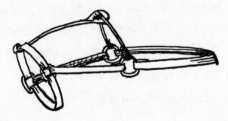

10. Victory

THE next day Pony called at Mr. George's apartment in Arcadia. The two were going to drive back to the ranch together.

"Where's your bag, Pony?" Mrs. George asked him as she let him into the living room.

"I don't need one," he said. He didn't want to tell her that he had always carried his few belongings around in a sack.

"But what do you carry your clothes in?" she wanted to know.

"I only got a pair of jeans and a shirt extra," Pony explained.

"But where are they?" Mrs. George was very pretty, but Pony could see that for all her sweet, soft looks, she was not a woman one could get around easily.

He hung his head a moment. "I left them rolled up behind some plants in the hall downstairs."

Mrs. George turned without another word and went in search of her husband. "Harry!" Pony could hear her calling. "Harry!"

That is how it came about that a new suitcase full of clothing for Pony stood right alongside Mr. George's in the back part of the car when an hour later the two started on their way.

Pony leaned back against the leather cushions of the wide front seat and watched the wide land through which they were swiftly traveling. He knew it was the same highway he had traveled only a few days before. But today everything about it looked different to him. Today it seemed almost as if the land smiled back at him. It was hard to remember now, with Mr. George beside him and the thought of Little Vic ahead of him, that he had ever been lonely or downhearted.

One thing still troubled him, though. How would Joe Hills feel about his riding Little Vic? Pony had not told Mr. George that Joe Hills had not liked him on sight. He had let his new friend think that Joe Hills was only angry with him on account of Little Vic. Pony had tried several times to tell Mr. George the truth about Joe Hills. But somehow the words just could not get themselves spoken. He decided at last that what was wrong between him and Joe Hills was something one couldn't talk about even to a friend.

Mr. George hurried the trip and they arrived at the ranch the next day. He had sent no word of his coming, and it was a very surprised Honey who turned from her stove to see the two of them walk into her kitchen.

At first she was too astonished to say a word. Then a wide smile split her kind, brown face. "You did it!"

she said in a wondering voice. Her eyes were shining. "You did it! You found him!"

"He sure did, Honey," said Mr. George. "Now I've brought him home to help Joe and me get Little Vic ready for the big race."

Honey wasn't interested in Little Vic or races. But she had caught one very important word in what Mr. George had said. She wanted to be sure the boy had caught it too.

"Welcome home, Pony," she said.

Though he didn't reply, Pony thought those two words the loveliest he had heard in a long, long time.

Now Honey became her old busy self again. She flew about the kitchen getting supper on the table. "Like as not you been driving like a fast train, only on a train you got a chance to eat," she said crossly as she filled two big plates with cold chicken and then made coffee.

"We're hungry all right," Harry George told her, "but I wish you would give me fifteen minutes before you put it all on the table. I want to say 'hello' to Joe Hills. You stay here, Pony, and help Honey if she needs you."

Honey waited until Mr. George had left the kitchen,

then she turned quickly to Pony. "You know what?" she began. Pony shook his head, his eyes big with questioning. "Something here," Honey continued, laying a hand on her heart, "something right down here tells me he smells a rat."

"What do you mean?" asked Pony.

"He wants to see Joe alone," Honey explained.

Still Pony looked as if he didn't understand.

"I think Mr. George knows how Joe feels about you," Honey told him. "I think he's gone to straighten things out before Joe gets a chance to meet you again. Mr. George will make everything right. You'll see. Now tell me what happened after you left here."

She grabbed a bread knife and began cutting pieces of fresh white bread while Pony told her quickly about meeting Mr. George and winning the race with Sun Alarm.

Honey seemed not at all surprised at his good luck. "I had a hunch," she said. "I said a prayer for you every night you were gone. And right after I would get through saying the prayer, a verse would come into my head. It was always the same verse." She stopped halfway across the kitchen and stood very still. Her eyes were deep and filled with a strange brightness.

" 'Some trust in chariots, and some in horses; but we will remember the name of the Lord our God.' That's what the verse was. I knew it was the Lord telling me that because I put my faith in something higher than horses, my prayers for you would be answered. And they were. So let that be a lesson to you in future."

A new light had come into Honey's eyes as she spoke those last words to Pony. It was a sharp, almost a fierce light, and the boy, feeling that glance upon him, was almost frightened by Honey's serious face. It started him to thinking in a way that he had never done before. Was it Little Vic or Honey's God which had brought about, his new happiness? he asked himself. Or were they one and the same thing? He had learned from his mother that God was in everything; that all living things were God's creatures. Little Vic, then, no less than himself. Himself no less than Joe Hills.

There came the sound of footsteps on the back porch. The kitchen door opened, and Harry George and Joe Hills entered. Pony felt a sudden desire to get out of the room. But before he could quite disappear, he heard his name called.

"Pony," Joe Hills was saying in a perfectly friendly

144

voice, "Harry has been telling me about the race you rode on Sun Alarm. Seems like I should of known a jockey when I saw one." He walked across the kitchen to where Pony stood rooted in astonishment. "Sorry I was so rough on you the other night," he said, putting out his hand to the boy.

Pony could hardly believe his ears. This man was actually telling him, Pony, that he was sorry, and offering his hand too! He looked hard into Joe Hills' face. Though the man's mouth wore a thin smile, there was no smile in his hard blue eyes. Those eyes made Pony look away quickly, and his own gaze came to rest on the face of Mr. George. Slowly the man moved his head up and down, and Pony reached out to take Joe Hills' hand.

"It's okay, Mr. Hills," said Pony. "I didn't have any business taking Little Vic that night."

A slow, soft voice followed this remark with, "We like first names around here, Pony. At least for anyone wearing my silks," said Harry George. "From now on he's Joe, I'm Harry."

The next morning bright and early the two men were on hand to watch Pony work out Little Vic. It was a great thrill for the boy to be in the saddle again on Little Vic's back. He leaned forward to pat the smooth neck.

"You got to show them something this morning, fellow," he told the horse. And Little Vic dropped his head and danced a couple of quick side steps to show he understood.

His time for short distances was not good, however. The next morning they would run him a mile, Harry said, and if Little Vic didn't show anything then, he might change his mind about taking him to California.

But the next morning, working a mile and better, Little Vic clipped three seconds off the best time of any horse Harry had. "He's a distance runner, all right," he told Pony. "We'll work him a few more days before we start for Santa Anita."

A week later Little Vic was shipped to California. Pony insisted on riding with him in the freight car.

"But Pony," Harry George said, laughing, "I have stable boys to take over that job. You're a jockey now."

"I'm not *a* jockey," Pony informed him. "I'm Little Vic's jockey. Also his stable boy and exercise boy and anything else he needs from anybody. He'll make the trip in better shape if I go along with him.

And he's got to be in the best shape from now on if he's going to win the 'Cap."

Harry laughed again. "All right, Pony. Have it your way. If you would rather travel with Little Vic than with Joe and me, it's your business, I guess."

So Little Vic got his first sight of Santa Anita's stables with Pony Rivers right beside him. As usual when anything unusual happened to him, Little Vic seemed to take it all in his long stride. He walked quietly to his stall, stopping only for a good look around. His eyes seemed to rest longest on the mountains, and Pony let him take them in.

"Seems to have an eye for beauty anyway," one of the stable boys remarked.

Pony led Little Vic into his stall without letting on that he had heard the laughter which followed.

Of course everyone connected with the track thought Harry George must be crazy to enter a horse in the Handicap which had never won a race. Add to that the fact that the horse in question was going to be ridden by a boy who had not been a jockey for a year, and it became certain that another good horseman had gone off the deep end. In vain Pony told everyone who would listen that Little Vic was great. In

vain he reminded them that Little Vic was the son of the great Victory. They, in turn, reminded him of the colt's record. Then Pony had nothing to say, for it would have been useless to tell them of Little Vic's race that time he had won. Some people won't believe anything unless it can all be put down in black and white. "You're going up against *horses* in the 'Cap, kid," they told him. "Great horses. *And great riders.* You haven't got a prayer."

"Remember, he's no quarter horse," Harry kept

telling the boy. "Don't start him like one. Give him time. Maybe he's a stretch runner."

Joe Hills had wanted Harry to enter Little Vic in a race or two before the 'Cap. But Pony would have none of it.

"He isn't the kind of horse that will run just to be running. Little Vic won't put himself out unless it matters. It's got to be a big race. Honest, Harry, I've seen him before. When it was the flood, okay, so he ran. When he's up against horses like High Dollar and Sun Soldier and Ten Spot, he'll run all right. He knows when a race is worth him. Save him for the big one. He's that kind of a horse."

So Harry let it go at that.

One morning, two days before the race, a certain sports writer was leaning on the rail when Little Vic flew past the half-mile post. After the workout the man wrote a report of what he had seen for his paper. Next morning another sports writer joined the first one. They approached Harry George after the workout.

"He looks like a race horse to me," the first one said.

"That's what I bought him for," returned Harry quietly.

"Who's going to ride him?" asked the other reporter.

"The kid you saw working him this morning."

"Oh, no!" they both cried. "Give the horse a chance."

"That's what I aim to do," returned Harry still quietly and walked away from the two reporters, who watched him go as people watch after a man who is sick and cannot be cured.

At last the big Saturday was upon them, and with it the running of the Santa Anita Handicap. That would be the fourth race of the afternoon. By one o'clock there were over sixty thousand people at the track. They all looked forward to the fourth race when the greatest horses of the country would race for a prize amounting to nearly a hundred thousand dollars. At least that is what all the people supposed the horses to be racing for. They didn't know that one of the horses, and not a well-known one at all, was not racing for the prize. Little Vic was racing to prove that he was a worthy son of his great father. He wasn't just a race horse trying to win a stake. He was racing for his honor, the highest stake that horse, or man, can ever win. Anyway, that is what Pony thought, and

in his love for the horse he was sure that Little Vic
actually felt the same way about it.

Now Pony was taking his last instructions from Mr.
George. "Don't start him too fast, but don't let anything get too far ahead of you."

"Good luck," said Joe Hills, his face full of doubt.

"Thanks," said Pony and went off to the judges'
stand to weigh in.

And now he and Little Vic were in the long line
of horses following the pink-coated man on the gray
pony. It seemed very quiet on the track in spite of the
huge crowd. Overhead the sky held not a single cloud.
The mountains rose clear and blue off to the right,
and the sun was warm on Pony's back. The track
would be fast, he was thinking, just the kind of a track
Little Vic liked.

High Dollar made trouble in the starting gate and
it took several minutes to get the horses quieted for
the start. But at last the starter gave the signal, the gates
sprang open, and the race was on.

Many times during the weeks Pony had been getting
ready for this moment he had wondered how he would
feel when it was actually at hand. Would he be scared
because this was a great race with great horses and

great riders? Or would he be able to forget that fact
and ride as if it were just another country fair race?
But now that the moment was upon him he never
thought of these things at all. He thought only of the
horses passing him on each side. He saw only the backs
of the jockeys out in front, Little Vic's ears laid back,
and his blowing mane. The pace set by Ten Spot was
fast—terribly fast. Already most of the field had passed
Pony. But Little Vic was not a fast starter and there
was a mile and a quarter to go.

Suddenly Pony saw a hole on the outside. Did he
guide the colt to it, or had Little Vic seen it at the
same time, knowing by some sixth horse sense that he
must flash into it? At any rate, he sprang for that small
opening, nosing out High Dollar. Neck and neck the
two raced to the quarter pole. Then Little Vic drew
steadily ahead. At the halfway mark there were still
three horses in front of Pony, and again High Dollar
was making a bid to overtake him.

Now Pony began to talk to Little Vic, leaning low
on the horse's neck, and not knowing that he spoke.
It was as if his heart had begun to talk out loud. "You
can do it, fellow. You got to do it. It's for Victory,
Victory, *Victory!*"

Victory

The words were a shout lost in the pounding of those swift feet, in the rush of air through wide nostrils. But like a horse with wings, Little Vic seemed suddenly to skim the ground in great leaps that put High Dollar a length behind him. Slowly he drew past the horse in third place and moved up on Sun Soldier. Ten Spot was still out in front. But as the horses came into the stretch Ten Spot, having set the pace so far, began to tire. Slowly he dropped back, and it became a race between Little Vic and Sun Soldier.

The people in the grandstand had risen to their feet. They yelled because they couldn't keep from yelling. Down the stretch they came, two great horses almost neck and neck, one bright bay, the other a dark brown. One already famous, the other until this moment unknown, but from this moment never to be forgotten while men lived who could believe in the triumph of faith over heavy odds. For it was the darker horse which crossed the finish line first. Little Vic was the winner by a head of the Santa Anita Handicap.

It wasn't until he was trotting back to the winner's circle that Pony became really aware of the crowd. It was cheering like mad. His first thought was that all that noise would frighten Little Vic. Then Harry

George stepped up to put his hand on the horse's bit. "Well, Pony," was all he said, but his smile was full of pride for what Pony had done. His eyes were deep and warm, like a father's eyes when he looks upon a son who has done well.

"It wasn't me," Pony said in answer to that look. "It was Little Vic."

"We'll let it go at that," said Harry George, smiling.

He led his horse into the winner's circle. Now, for the first time, Little Vic, his head high, his ears pointed forward, and his nostrils wide, posed for a victory picture. It will never be known what he thought. But Pony's mind was going back to a certain moonlight night a few weeks ago when once before Little Vic had stood in a winner's circle after proving himself great. Pony was proud of this moment, proud that the horse he loved had shown himself to be a worthy son of his father. The time for the race had gone up on the board in front of the grandstand. Little Vic had run the 'Cap in record time, as had his father many years before. It was good to know that here, before thousands of people, Little Vic had proved his greatness beyond the shadow of a doubt. Pony had wanted that for the colt. But now that it had been done, winning the 'Cap didn't seem to matter beside another victory. Always, for Pony, Little Vic's greatest race would be that other one which had been run on the edge of a draw when the stake had been the lives of several people.

The boy's eyes rested upon the great circle of flowers which had been placed around the horse's neck. But he remembered a night when Little Vic had been a horse with thunder on his neck. Tomorrow the papers would talk about a new wonder horse which had proved himself great in his first great race. Only Pony would know how wrong they were. Pony and Little Vic.

The newsmen finally left. The people crowding around the winner's circle drifted back to the grandstand to watch the next race. Little Vic was taken back to his stall. Pony took off his riding things, and started on his way to the stable, to be sure, before he joined the Georges in their box, that Little Vic was entirely all right.

Many thoughts were going through Pony's mind as he walked toward the stables. All his dreams had come true. His future with Little Vic was sure and certain. Harry had already promised that. It was all

Pony wanted. It was all he had asked for. He should have been perfectly happy. But he wasn't. The reason was Joe Hills.

How could he be happy around a man who didn't like him? Pony asked himself. And what could he do about it? What could anyone do to win the friendship of a man who had hated you on sight, and who still hated you in spite of everything? Joe Hills was the only person connected with the stable who had not had a kind word for Pony after the 'Cap. Joe Hills had disappeared almost as soon as the race was over and hadn't shown himself to Pony since. Maybe he hated him worse than ever for daring to win the race at all, Pony thought, dreading the moment when they would have to meet.

The first man he saw on approaching the George stable was Joe Hills.

"Hello, Pony," said the man.

There was nothing in Joe's voice to tell Pony what he might be thinking.

"Hi, Joe," said Pony, and walked straight on toward Little Vic's stall.

"Pony!" The sharpness of Joe's voice stopped the boy. Slowly he turned around to face the man. "Pony,

Victory

I waited to talk to you because there's something I got to get off my chest."

Pony could feel the blood draining out of his face. His mouth felt suddenly dry. For the first time since the race he realized he was very, very tired. His knees seemed to have lost their strength. He longed to sit down, but there was no place to sit. There was nothing he could do but stand here facing Joe Hills and wait for whatever might follow. If only he hadn't run into the man. Pony didn't want any trouble. Not today. He didn't want anything to spoil today.

"Can't it wait till tomorrow, Joe?" In spite of himself, Pony's voice shook a little.

"No, it can't," returned Joe firmly. "I may not want to say it tomorrow, and it's got to get said." He was silent for a moment, as if gathering his words together to look carefully at them before he spoke. At last he looked straight into Pony's troubled brown eyes. "I been brought up to think every white person is better than every colored person. My father was brought up the same way, and his father before him. I can't shed that idea all at once because I've had it too many years. I know it don't make sense, but there it is, and there don't seem to be nothing I can do about it."

157

Little Vic

"You don't have to tell me this, Joe. It's okay," Pony started to say. But the man held up a silencing hand and the boy waited unhappily for him to finish.

"You got to hear me out because I ain't never going to talk about it again. Today you did something I couldn't have done. Not the riding," he said hurriedly. "I'd have been a jockey myself if I hadn't been so big. l love horses. The way you love them." His eyes lifted for a moment to meet the boy's. "Only I couldn't never believe in any horse the way you believe in Little Vic. I just don't believe that much in anything. I guess it's a good thing to believe that much in something, but it just ain't in my makeup." He thought a moment. "I know it's a good thing because it's all that brought you through. You had everything against you, but you won because you love that horse more than anything. More than yourself."

He stopped speaking for so long that Pony wondered if he had finished what he wanted to say. But Joe had more to say and his face showed plainly what a struggle it cost him to get the words out.

"Once I shook your hand because Harry told me if I didn't he'd fire me. I hated myself that day, and I

158

ain't been feeling too comfortable ever since." Now his eyes met Pony's once again, and this time their gaze was steady. "I'd like to shake hands with you now because I think you're a great little guy."

Pony felt as if he had just wakened out of a bad dream. But he hadn't dreamed what Joe had just said. There was the man standing in front of him, looking suddenly shy and awkward, his hand reaching out toward Pony. Still unable to say a word, the boy moved forward and their hands met. As their glances met and held, and their clasp tightened, Pony suddenly found his tongue. "Let's have a look at Little Vic together," was what he said.

For answer, Joe smiled and started toward the stall. Pony swung along beside him, his thoughts busy with a surprising discovery. He was knowing again, right now, the same lifted-up feeling he had known on the night of Little Vic's greatest race. Was this meeting with Joe another kind of victory? And if so, whose was it? Was it possible to share a victory equally? Had he and Joe both won?

When they got to the stall each one took a side of Little Vic and from long habit began running their hands over him.

At last Joe said, "Now we got to think about the Run for the Roses."

Pony jerked himself up straight. "You think Harry will run him in the Derby?"

"Sure," said Joe quietly. "Didn't he tell you?"

For a moment Pony was silent as he took in the importance of this news. Then he said slowly, "It's right for Little Vic to make good in his father's country, in the blue grass. Because he's going to win the Derby."

"He will if you ride him," returned Joe.

"I'll ride him," said Pony.

Over the back of the horse they both loved their eyes met, and they smiled at each other as people smile who have just made a great discovery—together.